WE ALL FALL DOWN

- Stories of Plague and Resilience -

ISBN: 978-1939138217

Edited by J.K. Knauss

Cover designed by Mirella Patzer

Featuring Stories By

David Blixt, Jean Gill, Kristin Gleeson,
J. K. Knauss, Laura Morelli, Katherine Pym,
Deborah Swift, Melodie Winawer, and Lisa J. Yarde

Publicity Contact
Lisa J. Yarde
lisa@lisajyarde.com
www.lisajyarde.com

Dedication

To Katherine Pym,
A dedicated writer and contributor to this anthology,
who lives each day to the fullest with courage and
determination.

FOREWORD

By Lisa J. Yarde

Throughout history, humans have endured the ravages of epidemic diseases and pestilence. Arguably, no such catastrophe in the historical record has claimed more lives than the bubonic plague, more commonly known as the Black Death, during the Middle Ages in Europe. The origins and virulent causes for so much death have been debated for centuries, but the scale of the devastation and its impact on history have not. Particularly during the fourteenth century, in the deserts of Asia Minor and across the Middle East and North Africa, to the shores of the Mediterranean Sea, the Balkans, the Iberian Peninsula, populous cities within France, and Germany, and northward to the British Isles, Norway, Denmark, Sweden, the Baltic countries and even Russia, the Black Death ravaged the land. Latin physicians called it *pestilentia*. In Northern Europe, the term was *plaga*, which came into modern English usage as "plague." Other sources referred to it as the Great Mortality. Aided by general filth, poor sanitation, and the free flow of trade, whole families died off. No such catastrophic demographic decline, estimated by Dr. Ole J. Benedictow, at up to 50 million or 60 percent of fourteenth-century Europe's population, had been previously recorded in history.

Deaths from bubonic plague were brutal. Painful buboes appeared on the groin, thigh, armpit, or neck of infected persons. Within three to five days of these signs of infection, victims spat blood, had seizures and terrible coughs, and their skin turned black as the flesh necrotized. The disease spared no one; kings and nobility perished as did merchants, sailors, and the poor. Since the Middle Ages, the plague has reoccurred in every subsequent century. While its spread abated, people remained in fear of the next violent outbreak. Such disease still haunts our lives. As recently as 1993, fears of an epidemic caused the flight of one million inhabitants from the Indian city of Surat, almost half of the population.

What was it like for our ancestors to endure such a calamity? -Did victims turn to religion or medical practitioners, or surrender to despair? How many people survived the aftermath of the disease and how were their lives altered? Did doctors realize that the same epidemic had recurred across the centuries? With each incidence, what medical and scientific advances had emerged to combat the plague?

The nine authors of this anthology—David Blixt, Jean Gill, Kristin Gleeson, J. K. Knauss, Laura Morelli, Katherine Pym, Deborah Swift, Melodie Winawer, and Lisa J. Yarde—have imagined how the bubonic plague claimed its earliest victims, the desolation left in its wake, and how survivors rebuilt shattered lives. These are more than unique stories of horrific pain, loss, and death. The collection is bound together by universal themes of hope, love, and courage, a powerful testament to humanity's fortitude.

Like the wide swathe of the Black Death's spread, the stories range across various periods and places, from fourteenth-century Tuscany, Ireland, Spain, and Italy, to Venice in the sixteenth century, seventeenth-century England and Scotland, and the Ottoman-influenced Mediterranean region. Each tale is as exceptional as the impact of the plague on the characters' lives.

Meet Little Bird, who travels on a wagon across medieval Tuscany with a band of fraudster "cure sellers" hawking their wares at a time when the Black Death takes the lives of increasing numbers of Sienese. In fourteenth-century Ireland, young Maeve's faith is tested as she faces grave choices in the care of her ailing father, which may cause her abandonment of her convent home. In two stories from medieval Spain, Leonor, the lover of a king, lives in peril at the mercy of a jealous queen during the aftermath of Alfonso XI's death by plague, while the Moorish doctor Ibn al-Khatib seeks more knowledge about the disease at great personal cost. Meanwhile, in medieval Italy, Pietro, son of the famed writer Dante, contemplates whether his father's epic tale in *The Inferno* is a cruel allegory for lives ruined by the Black Death.

Then, the artist Titian endures the likelihood of obscurity in a place designated for disease sufferers and his eventual demise, as the pestilence descends on Venice in the sixteenth century. There are two seventeenth-century tales set in the British Isles, where the wily Scottish thief Finn O'Donnell suffers the death of his father through plague and loss of the familial home, and London physician Nathaniel Hodges undertakes the care of victims in a deserted city, while facing the possible loss of one of his apprentices to the epidemic. In seventeenth-century Greece, occupied by the Ottoman Empire, the Turk Kadri bin Ahmed comes of age just before the invasion of a Venetian fleet and the arrival of plague in his homeland brings the grim prospect of death.

At the end of each story, authors share their inspiration for the particular tale. These are more than macabre accounts of the tragic losses suffered by plague victims. Characters evoke resolve and determination in their will to endure the disease. We hope readers will be inspired by these fictionalized lives.

The Blood of the Gaels

By Kristin Gleeson

Clyde, 1348

Desperation. That's what Maeve heard in the prayers all around her. Though she clasped her hands just as tightly in prayer as the others, endured the pain in her knees and closed her eyes tight, the words wouldn't come. Could their founding abbess, the blessed Gobnait, really hold back the tide of this most dangerous plague that was edging ever closer to their convent? Despite all their efforts, the scourge continued to make its way west from Cork, first piercing the defences of the Normans in their proud stone manor homes to strike them dead and then to the lesser tenants. Would their prayers protect the Gaels?

The singing began and Maeve joined in gladly. It was the singing that kept her moving through her day, kept her kneeling with the others until she was allowed to go and tend her bees and blend the healing ointments, draughts, and herbal remedies for the sick who requested it at the convent. Would these remedies, ointments, and draughts have any effect if the prayers failed and the plague did come? She didn't know.

These doubts she had were voiced only in her head and had been slipping through the cracks and holes of her daily routine in this community of women.

The prayers came to an end and, as if by some secret signal, the women rose in unison, the walls of the small stone church still echoing the recent chants of Prime. The women filed towards the door, where the weak winter morning light filtered in. Maeve pulled her novice's habit closer around her, bracing herself against the blustery rain that had come with the dawn. Before she reached the door, the abbess touched her arm.

"Daughter, will you stay a moment? I would like to speak with you."

"Of course."

They both waited while the few remaining women filed out. When the last one had disappeared, the abbess took Maeve's hand and gave her a considered look.

"Maeve, I've had word from your family. I'm afraid the news is not good."

Maeve braced herself, clutching the abbess's hand. "Is it my mother? Is she ill?" Her mother had suffered ill health when Maeve was young, before her family had pledged her to this community, as had been the daughters of countless generations of her family from the time when Gobnait founded the community. So her mother had told her.

"Your mother is well," said the abbess. "I'm afraid it's your father."

"My father?" It seemed impossible that her always healthy parent who'd often been compared to a bull should be ill. "Has he met with some sort of accident? Is he injured?"

"No. He has fallen ill with some ailment. Your mother isn't certain. But she asks that you come and nurse him."

"Ailment?" She tried to keep her voice calm. "Does she suspect...." The words hung in the air, but there was no question about Maeve's meaning.

"She doesn't say. But you must be prepared for anything."

"I will go to her immediately." Maeve paused and lowered her eyes. "With your permission, of course, Mother Abbess."

The abbess's expression turned grave. "My child, it is more than a question of fulfilling your duty to your parents. There are other things to consider. If it be plague that ails your father, it is a serious matter, not just to ensure that his soul is addressed, but—"

"I will be fine," said Maeve. "And, as you have said, it hasn't affected the Gaels." She studied the Abbess. "That is

2

still the case, is it not?"

The abbess hesitated. "I'm not certain, but I believe so." The abbess's confident manner seemed to have disappeared under the weight of Maeve's situation, which made Maeve more uncertain about what she should do. She thought of her father, who had been so doting towards her in the years she'd been at home, and had voiced objections to the plan to send Maeve to the community here in Borneach, arguing that Maeve's older sister was much more suited to the life than Maeve. But her mother had won out, claiming that she couldn't bear to lose her oldest daughter who was such a comfort and had already contracted a good marriage.

"My child, you must do what you think best. You aren't yet fully pledged to God and this community."

The abbess reached up and touched Maeve's cheek. Her naturally pale cheeks, framed even with her head cover by escaping russet curls, grew paler. Maeve braced herself for the words to come.

"I must warn you, though," said the abbess, "that when you leave here, it may not be possible for you to return."

For a moment she was stunned. All those prayers they'd offered up, now it was clear the abbess had as little faith in them as she did if she thought Maeve would carry plague on her return. Was it so very much a sacrifice for her not to return?

"We will pray for you, child. Should you decide to go. But you have a duty to your father. You must ask God for guidance."

Maeve searched the abbess's face. She glimpsed the fear behind the compassion and the studied calm. The reassurance and comfort she had always derived from the strong presence of the abbess through the years as she'd struggled with her vocation disappeared. She suppressed the spark of anger that ignited in her and took a deep breath.

"There is no need for prayer," she said. "I will go."

The abbess seemed to sense her suppressed anger. "We

serve God, the highest purpose of all, and it's that I must protect first and foremost," she said in a firm and cool tone.

"Of course, Mother Abbess. I understand." She understood enough to know that God's will was something she could never comprehend, least of all now.

The horse plodded heavily on the rutted track. Maeve shifted slightly, trying to ease the numbness that had settled in all her lower extremities. Her arms tightened instinctively around the waist of her companion, Diarmuid. "Shall we take our ease for a spell, sister? There's a clearing up ahead," he said.

"Yes, thank you," she said, startled. She'd had few words from Diarmuid since they'd departed the community several hours before. She was grateful to him and thankful, too, that the abbess had at least given her this man as an escort. He'd recently arrived at the community and was one of the workers who helped with the animals and the farm that supported the sisters. He was closer in age to Maeve than the other men that worked there and wasn't a local man, either. His dark curls and brawny appearance marked him as the Kerry man he was. But she knew nothing more about him, his family, or clan, only his name.

Now, as he handed her down from the horse, she studied his face that showed only a carefully schooled expression. She wondered if he knew the exact nature of her journey and the probable consequences that would affect him as much as it would her. She could only suppose that he did, for she couldn't imagine the abbess being other than truthful for something so important. Would he stay with her at her home, or return to his own? And would her family welcome him?

He caught her studying him and she thought then she detected a hint of amusement. She lowered her eyes and noticed that his hands weren't as work-roughened as she would expect of someone that had laboured manually all his life. In fact, they were rather elegantly tapered, except for the missing part of the third finger she suddenly noticed. Her eyes widened. She looked up again at him and he raised a brow, his eyes no longer hiding the humour. She flushed.

He dismounted without a word and withdrew a small cloth bundle containing food from their pack. Maeve found a large rock to perch on, safe from the wet grass, and took the cloth bundle that he handed to her.

"I'll just take the horse to the river over there beyond that cluster of trees."

Maeve nodded and busied herself unfastening the bundle and laying out food for herself and Diarmuid. The horse's hooves and the rustle of branches signalled his return a short while later. She gestured to Diarmuid to sit and then saw the concerned look on his face.

"What is it?"

He glanced over at her, his blue eyes darkening for a moment. He forced a smile. "Nothing, I'm sure."

"Nothing didn't cause that expression."

His smile widened a little, and this time a touch of humour showed in his eyes. "There were a few pigs and a cow loose, drinking at the river."

"Loose animals are cause for concern?"

"There was no sign of anyone nearby. No farmer of any worth would allow that. The animals are just too valuable in these times."

"You're right, of course."

Maeve mentally berated herself for her ignorant comment. She'd spent so many years in the protected confines of the community that she'd forgotten so much of what came naturally to others whose lives revolved around the land and the elements. She could only hope that the time she'd spent with the bees, mixing healing medicaments and tending the sick, would help her with what was to come. But she considered his statement carefully and realized that the words that remained unspoken were even more important. What had become of the farmer, his family, and clan that could cause animals to remain loose?

"There's probably an innocent explanation," she said with deliberate calm. She handed him a chunk of cheese and some oatcakes.

"Yes," said Diarmuid, his tone neutral. He remained standing, took the proffered food, but didn't eat.

She stiffened, reading his implied directive to leave immediately, with a flash of anger, but forced herself to concede the wisdom of it. "We'll make for the Uí Chartaigh holding near Archad Dorbchon as soon as we can. There, hopefully, we'll hear if there is any plague along the way."

Diarmuid nodded. "We should take care along the way, sister."

They packed up the small bundle and soon were on their way. Maeve's senses seemed more keenly attuned now, and she heard the soughing of the wind through the trees that sent the winter birds into flight. She started several times at each new sound until Diarmuid spoke.

"All will be well, sister."

"You must call me Maeve. I am not yet pledged."

"Maeve," he said softly.

It was like music when he said her name, and together with the touch of his hand she somehow felt comforted.

From a distance, all seemed fine. Cows were grazing just outside the fort and she could make out a few sheep scattered in the next field. A fine mist was settling in, but Maeve knew that didn't explain the lack of people.Diarmuid halted the horse. "Stay here," he said and slid off the horse.

He approached the threshold of the stone building cautiously. In mid-stride he stopped, held his cloak across his mouth and nose and proceeded more cautiously, until he reached the threshold. It was only a few moments later that Maeve smelled the odour, too. Putrefaction. She gagged and forced herself to dismount and move forward.

"Stay there," said Diarmuid sharply.

"No. I'm a healer. I must see if there is anything I can do."

"There's nothing to be done. They're all dead."

Maeve glanced around her again, noting the cows that stood shuffling only a little under her scrutiny. "But that's impossible, surely. Even the milk cows are recently tended." That much she did remember of husbandry. As if to deny her statement, a painful lowing sounded.

"They must have only recently fallen ill. The illness wastes little time," said Diarmuid.

She saw the compassion and pain in his eyes as he looked inside once again. It was only brief, and when he turned to face her, his expression was firm. "There's no reason for you to come any closer." He blocked the door as if he knew what she meant to do.

"You don't understand. I must at least view the bodies to determine if it be the plague and if so, that I can increase my knowledge of this disease." She paused and added in a low voice. "For the sake of my father."

He studied her carefully and she bore his scrutiny, trying to appear calmly determined. After a moment he sighed and moved aside. "You will see enough here, from the door."

She pulled her cloak across her mouth and nose and, bracing herself, approached the entrance. It took a few moments for her eyes to adjust. The room was large with several chairs and benches, storage chests and a large trestle table against one wall, all surrounding a central hearth. Makeshift pallets had been created and placed on one side of the room, as if the effort to climb the stairs to the floor above to the more comfortable living quarters was too much effort. And on each of these makeshift pallets lay a body. Three children and three adults, one of them elderly. The only woman was fully clothed, the front of her gown stained with blood and vomit, as were the sleeping shifts of the others. A woeful sight that brought tears to Maeve's eyes.

"You're right, it does strike quickly," said Maeve. "But they show no evidence of the pustules, the blackened fingers and toes that I've heard reported. Could it be something else?"

"Possibly, but it seems just as deadly." He laid a hand on her shoulder. "Come, we should go. We'll find a way to let someone know so they can be buried. It's clear we can't stay here tonight."

She paused, overwhelmed by the devastation. "A prayer first?" she said in a low voice. "For their souls."

"A prayer outside. Surely the Lord will hear it just as well."

She assented. Was it because she agreed with him, or was it because she wondered if the Lord heard her prayers at all? Or any of the sisters at the community. But perhaps it was a punishment from God for their sins. That had seemed reasonable when applied to the Normans who sought to extend their occupation of Ireland. But these people were Gaels. Was that part of God's plan?

She sighed and followed Diarmuid back to the horse. She paused, closed her eyes and offered a prayer, hoping that it would be heard.

Her leg muscles were sore, but it was her back that caused her to stretch now and shift slightly on the horse. A night spent huddled in a meagre, hastily constructed shelter hadn't helped. No matter the ascetic life she'd led in Teampall Gobnatan, she wasn't used to rough living, especially in winter. Even the small fire Diarmuid had managed and sharing the warmth of his thick cloak and hers hadn't warmed her enough. It was only when, feeling her shiver, Diarmuid took her in his arms that she'd felt warm. And the heat that arose in her body seemed nothing to do with the gesture, but rather as a result of her emotions that his touch evoked. Now, she was conscious of her arms clutching his muscled abdomen. She made an effort to loosen her hold."You'll be able to ease yourself soon," said Diarmuid, feeling her shift. "The journey is nearly finished."

She looked around, surprised, and realized that she recognized the surroundings.

"Has it been long since you left your home?" asked Diarmuid.

She considered a moment. "Eight years. I'd just had my tenth summer when I arrived at Teampall Gobnatan." She paused and decided to finally ask what she'd wondered since they first began the journey. "What brought you to the community? You appear educated and from a good family. Surely you should have joined a monastery rather than laboured for a women's religious community."

Diarmuid gave a brief laugh. "It's not so much a desire to serve God that brought me there, rather a wish lead a quiet life with animals for company more often than humans."

Suddenly she felt ashamed of her unabashed curiosity and assumptions. "I'm sorry, I didn't mean to pry."

He smiled warmly and she could feel the colour rise in her face. "There's no need to apologize," he said. "It's natural that you should want to know more about me."

She waited for him to continue, but he remained silent. She resisted the urge to ask him more.

Soon they turned up the track to her home. She could see the sheep in the small hillside above the stone enclosure that surrounded the tower house. It had once been a proud home that had served the clan for generations. Now, the enclosure was crumbling in places, fences sagged, and the pens and fields were only sparsely populated with animals, a legacy of the Norman attempts to expand their holdings beyond the confines of Cork and replacing clan ownership with tenancies that demanded periodic tributes. In the west, the old ways still held, but here, closer to Cork, it was not so.

9

Maeve saw no sign of anyone outside her home and she was just beginning to fear the worst when a woman emerged from the house. Her mother. Her usually neat attire was crumpled, her headdress askew.

"It's too late," her mother cried. "You're too late!"

Maeve's breath caught in her throat. "He's dead?"

"No, no, but nearly so. There's nothing to be done, I'm sure of it."

With Diarmuid's help, Maeve slid quickly from the horse and her mother led the way, leaving Diarmuid to tend the horse and bring in the packs. Her home was as she remembered it. The hearth for cooking, now sporting a feeble fire, the fur rugs on the floor, the tapestries hanging along the walls, along with her father's shield and other tools of war were in the same place. She noted even his sword was hung up, instead of at his side or its belt looped on a chair, as it used to be. There was no trace of her brother, his own sword gone, buried no doubt with him, after he'd been killed in some rebellious skirmish, some years before, defending the Gaels from Norman incursion.

She climbed the stairs to the upper chamber, where the loom, spindles and other domestic items were, as well as the comfortable seating and her parent's bed, curtained off from the rest of the room. She followed her mother through the parted curtain to where her father lay on the bed, pale and gaunt, his eyes shut. A male servant tended him, straightening the coverlet. He backed away when the two women entered.

Maeve rushed to her father's side, giving no thought to the contagion, her heart roused by the sight of him. She laid her hand on his chest and felt its shallow rise and fall and bent down and heard the faint breath from his mouth. She put a hand to his brow and could detect no strong fever, or anything else that might indicate plague.

"When did he fall ill?" she asked.

Her mother wrung her hands, her distress evident. "He wasn't feeling well. He had a slight fever so he took to his bed, maybe five or six days ago. I sent for you right away."

"Have you heard of any cases of plague nearby?"

"Not as such," said her mother, her tone a little defensive. "But a pedlar has come recently. I thought he might have brought it. And he's become worse. Slowly he's lost the use of his limbs, and now his breath is gone. I've been doing all I could, beef broth and even a honey posset as you once wrote was good for ailments, but all to no avail."

Her father opened his eyes and focussed on Maeve. He gave her a weak smile. "Maeve, my daughter. You've come," he said in a hoarse voice. He looked behind her and his face filled with relief. "And you've brought your betrothed with you."

Was her father delirious? Maeve checked behind her and saw Diarmuid standing close by, her healer's bundle in his hands. She opened her mouth to explain, but her father interrupted her.

"Come, give your father a proper greeting."

Puzzled, she leaned over him again and as she kissed his cheek, he whispered to her. "You must abandon your novitiate and save our holding by marrying the young man. There is no time to lose, for I haven't long."

Maeve stared at her father, trying to make sense of what he said. Was it his ailment? Clearly it wasn't the plague. She looked across at her mother and she could see fear in her eyes. Her mother hadn't bothered to contradict her father. Was something amiss, as he said?

"It's not the plague," Maeve said. She glanced at the servant who still lingered in the room, though his task was complete. "The servant is to be commended for his loyalty, though. That he should remain and tend his master with the fear of plague in the household. Have the other servants fled?"

Her mother nodded. "Those of the household."

The servant kept his head down and bowed low. "I will take my leave, now, my lady, and go tend the cows."

After he departed Maeve spoke. "He's not from our clan, is he? His speech is different."

"No," said her mother, distractedly. "He's only been here a short while. He helps with the heavy chores in the house and sometimes with the animals. He claims that his mother is somehow connected to our clan and after his wife died of some illness he came here because his own clan had lost their lands."

"No servant is that loyal, especially one newly joined the household," said Diarmuid. "Something is afoot."

"I fear so," said Maeve. She realized she was glad of his calm presence to help her face this undercurrent of misdeed that was visiting her home. She'd come to the conclusion that it was no usual illness that had taken her father. Not with his symptoms. He'd been poisoned.

Her mother knotted her gown anxiously. "You may be right. But how was I to attend anything with your father so ill?" she said, her voice plaintive. She glanced at Diarmuid. "Is it true what your father said? That this man is your betrothed? I was never told, but then, what is unusual about that?"

"She only recently wrote me the news, seeking my blessing," said her father. He gave Maeve a meaningful look.

Uncertain, Meave glanced at Diarmuid, his puzzlement clear. "I'm sorry, I've neglected to introduce you to Diarmuid," she said, playing for time. How was she to manage this situation? She made the introduction as best she could, but she realized she knew so little about him, not even his clan.

As if sensing her discomfort, Diarmuid moved forward and stood by her father's bed, next to Maeve. He rested a hand on Maeve's shoulder. "My father is Ua Donoghue Mor of Gleann Fleisce."

Her father's face brightened. "Yes, I remember now. A man with such standing, how could I refuse such an offer? And Patrick de Cogan and his steward could hardly object to such an alliance."

With the mention of the steward, her father's tone had become a sneer. Maeve opened her mouth to object, or at least question her father further, but he held up his hand and resumed speaking, his voice tired.

"Her dower lands will resort back, and if we can but draw up the documents now I will make you my heir, keeping the land within the clan, keeping it with the Gaels, if only as a tenancy, if you will take on the name."

"You're certain the tenancy will continue with us?" asked Maeve. It was all too quick, she could hardly think. She felt the pressure of Diarmuid's hand on her shoulder. He squeezed it. Marriages were sometimes made on much less. Was he really willing? Should she agree?

"It's his steward that's covets this land, this tenancy," he said, spitting. He looked at Diarmuid. "You will agree?"

"I feel you must know something more, before any documents are signed," said Diarmuid. "You may not feel the same."

With an effort, her father shook his head. "No, I'm sure I will."

"Nevertheless, I must tell you that though I am the oldest son, my younger brother is Tánaiste."

"It matters not that you won't be chief," said her father. "The lands of that region aren't in Norman hands and will then remain safe from them."

"The reason for this decision is because I killed a clan member in a fight. My uncle. I paid for it with banishment and," he held up his hand with the partial finger, "this."

Censure flickered across her father's face briefly but then was replaced by a smile. "I suspect there was good cause for that," he said. "Now, can I ask you to draw up the documents?"

Diarmuid looked at Maeve, a question in his eyes. She'd heard the exchange in silence, trying to reconcile all that she knew and had experienced of this man beside her. She knew what she felt at his touch, the humour in his eyes when it was present and the warmth of his embrace, if only to provide comfort or warmth. Would a man such as that kill his uncle for anything other than a just cause? A moment later she felt she knew her answer. She gave

Diarmuid a small nod.

The completed documents were laid before her father. Some parchment had been found and a quill and ink. Diarmuid, Maeve had discovered, had studied the law for a short time, another piece of knowledge about him that was surprising, and so was able to write the contract. With the two field labourers as witnesses, Diarmuid and Maeve helped hold the quill in her father's paralysed hand and make his mark that would serve as his signature. The labourers followed suit with their own mark.When the signatures were all made, Maeve's father spoke. "Get the sword."

Puzzled, she did as he requested. When she'd returned, sword in hand, she started to hand it to her father.

"No," he said. "Give it to Diarmuid. I want him to swear on the hilt, as he would any cross, that he will uphold the blood of the Gaels, the honour of this clan, and protect you with his life."

Silently, she handed the sword to Diarmuid and he placed his hand upon the hilt. The oath was made. The contract was complete. It remained only for her to pledge herself to him and they would be married. She looked in Diarmuid's eyes and squeezed her hand gently and smiled encouragement. She made her promise.

The ceremony complete, her father closed his eyes. "It's done," he whispered. His breathing was more laboured, as if he was ready to surrender to the death he'd been fighting since Maeve's arrival. A few moments later, his breath ceased.

Maeve fought back the tears and gave no resistance when Diarmuid drew her into his arms. Behind her, her mother set up a long sharp wail. It pierced Maeve's ears and she closed her eyes, willing her to stop. She allowed herself a few moments of the comfort of Diarmuid's embrace, then pulled away and straightened.

"Mother, you must get hold of yourself. There is much to be done."

Her mother gulped heavily, trying to control herself, and managed to lessen the wracking sobs that had succeeded the wails.

"We must wash the body," said Maeve, dismissing the field labourers to find the priest. "I'll just get the water and cloths," she told her mother as she exchanged a glance with Diarmuid.

Diarmuid followed her downstairs where an empty room faced them.

"That servant is gone," said Diarmuid. "I don't like it."

"Nor do I," said Maeve. "I feel certain he has something to do with my father's death. That was no ailment that killed him. He was poisoned. Belladonna, hellebore, or perhaps even hemlock." She glanced around the room. "I want to see if I can find anything here to confirm it."

Diarmuid gave her a grim look. "I'm going ride out and see if I can find that servant in the meantime."

She placed a hand on his arm and looked up into his very blue eyes, concerned. "Please, Diarmuid, take my father's sword. He would want you to have it, anyway. You may as well begin carrying it now."

He took the hand from his arm, held it up to his lips and kissed it. "I will do as you say, Maeve," he said softly.

The touch of his lips on her hand stirred something inside her. On impulse she reached up and kissed his cheek. "Go safely, and with God," she said.

He nodded and without further word, he scooped up the sword from the chair where Maeve had placed it and left.

Maeve wiped her father's brow and then his cheeks, the wet cloth tracing moisture in its wake, while her mother watched her with helpless distraction. Maeve tried to keep her thoughts focussed on her task, and not on the threat posed by the steward and whoever had murdered her father. She began to offer up a prayer for her father's soul, hoping it would help."I hear hoofbeats," said her mother, anxiously. "Someone's coming." She went to the window.

"It's probably the priest," Maeve said.

Though it was possible, she doubted the priest would be here already, but she didn't want to alarm her mother. She put down the cloth and joined her mother by the small window. She pulled aside the waxed cloth that covered the window and peered out. In the distance she could make out two riders, one wearing a surcoat with a device emblazoned on it. She frowned. A Norman.

Her mother peered out beside her and gasped. "It's the steward. What shall we do?"

Maeve bit her lip, badly regretting Diarmuid's absence. There was nothing for it, though, she must cope the best she could. She laid a calming hand on her mother's shoulder.

"We will go to greet him and offer him hospitality as any Gael would a visitor," she said. "Come, tidy yourself and we'll prepare for his arrival."

She ushered her mother to the floor below. The fire was nearly out, so she went to stir it, asking her mother to prepare a cup of warmed ale. By the time the visitors passed through the outer wall, Maeve was ready, her skirts brushed, and her headcloth firmly in place. She took her mother's hand and opened the door, ready with a greeting.

The steward dismounted gracefully, despite his bulk, his cropped fair hair shining in the fading afternoon light. In this time of the year, darkness would fall soon, a thought which made Maeve frown inwardly, for it would mean that it was likely the steward would call upon them to put him up for the night. She pasted a smile on her face and offered him the welcome cup and bade him come in. He took the cup and drank deeply. When he'd finished, he nodded and handed it back to her, eyeing her appreciatively.

"Thank you," he said in his own language. "Though I know your lady mother, I fear we have not met yet. Let me introduce myself, I am Guy de Harcourt, steward to Patrick de Cogan."

She nodded. It was some years since she'd even heard the language, and though she'd had some facility with the tongue, she knew that she must take care, and wait for the words to come.

"I am Maeve, daughter of Cormac Uí Fhlionn of Raithleann."

Her mother gave her welcome, her own efforts clumsy and ill pronounced, but the steward bowed nonetheless and seemed not to notice. He gestured to his companion and bade him stable his horse.

They entered the tower and Maeve offered Harcourt the best chair, now covered for comfort in fur skins and placed by the fire. She offered him some bread and cheese, the best her and her mother could assemble at such short notice. He held up his hand in refusal.

The two women stood in front of him expectantly. He looked from one to the other.

"I haven't come to exchange pleasantries," he said. "I've come to inquire after your father. I understand he's taken to his bed and is ill unto death."

Maeve exchanged looks with her mother, her mother's face filled with fear.

"My father died just a few hours ago."

De Harcourt looked surprised. "Did he? It seems I must offer my sympathies then."

"Thank you," said Maeve. Her mother stood in helpless silence slightly behind Maeve now, her fear almost palpable.

"With the event of your father's death without an heir, as steward for Patrick de Cogan, suzerain of this area, I must tell you that this tenancy reverts back to his lordship. And until such time as it is decided otherwise, I will take over the tenancy. "

"But there is an heir," Maeve said. She drew herself up to her full height.

"No," he said in a deliberate, kind tone. "With your brother dead, you pledged to the convent, your sister married and living with her husband's family, there is no heir."

"But I am no longer pledged. I won't be taking my vows. Didn't your informer tell you that?"

Harcourt's expression darkened for a moment, but he chose to ignore the comment. "But that will make matters simple. Your dower lands will revert to the tenancy and now that you're free to marry, we can arrange a contract for marriage with me. There will be no objection." He gave her a self-satisfied look.

Maeve regarded him with studied calm. "I fear my husband would object."

"Your husband? Is this an attempt at humour?"

"I assure you it is not."

Harcourt's lips curled into a sneer. "And just who is this husband and where is he?"

"He will return soon. He's attending to concerns that arose when my father died."

"How convenient," said Harcourt. He frowned. "I'm afraid I must challenge your assertion. Without any proof, my only choice is to take over this holding."

"But I have proof," said Maeve. She turned to her mother. "Can you fetch the contracts, please, mother?" she said quietly in their own language.

Her mother stared at her a moment, then nodded nervously. "Of course."

She hurried off up the stairs.

"This marriage is a recent occurrence, I presume," said Harcourt.

"It's legal, nonetheless," Maeve said firmly.

He gave her a lazy, assessing look that bordered on a leer. He placed a hand on the hilt of his sword that still hung at his side. Maeve tried to keep the disdain from her face, not wishing to aggravate him unnecessarily, but she wouldn't let him think he was intimidating her.

A few moments later, she heard her mother descending the stairs. Maeve studied Harcourt's face, but could see nothing that would lead her to believe he might accept the situation she presented. When her mother arrived, she handed the documents to Harcourt. He scanned them quickly, his brow furrowed. When he'd finished, he stood, rolled up the contracts and placed them inside the padded tunic underneath his hauberk and surcoat.

"I'll take these to Patrick de Cogan and see what he says," he told her.

Maeve held out her hand. "I would appreciate it if you would return the contracts to me now. We'll present them to Patrick de Cogan ourselves." She heeled his gaze, hoping her firm stance would be enough to make him comply.

His face was full of derision. "Oh, I think not."

She frowned. She had no doubt that he would destroy the contracts at the first opportunity. "There are witnesses that will attest to the existence of these contracts."

"Yes. And be sure I have noted who they are."

The door opened and Diarmuid entered, the sword still strapped at this side.

Though his clothes remained the same labourer's garments that he'd worn upon leaving Teampall Gobnatan, his demeanour had changed. His stance was that of a warrior, shoulders thrown back, feet apart, his hand on his sword hilt.

Relief flooded Maeve. She gave him a warm smile. "Husband, may I present Guy de Harcourt, Patrick de Cogan's steward," she said in the Norman tongue. "He seeks to take the tenancy, even though I presented him with the contracts of marriage and land disposition. He has chosen to take them from us, insisting he will deal with the matter himself, rather than allow us to present them to Patrick de Cogan ourselves after we have buried my father."

Diarmuid greeted Harcourt with a brief bow and moved close to Maeve, putting his arm around her shoulder. He rested the other hand on his sword.

"I fear Patrick de Cogan will not be pleased to hear the information I have gathered, which would prove his steward, a servant who is meant to uphold the lord's wishes, has in fact plotted the murder of one of his loyal tenants for his own ends. Patrick de Cogan wouldn't appreciate that his efforts to secure the land with Gaels loyal to him would be so disastrously undermined, for assuredly when word gets out, my own clan and others will join this clan and demand retribution, at the very least."

Harcourt drew his sword and moved towards Diarmuid, but Diarmuid already had his sword out and parried the blow that came, shoving Maeve out of the way. Harcourt attempted a few more blows, Diarmuid parried them equally well. Harcourt lowered his sword, visibly fighting to control his anger.

Diarmuid held out his hand. "The documents, Harcourt. Or will I have to take them by force?"

With a snarl, de Harcourt reached into his tunic, pulled out the rolled contracts and tossed them to Diarmuid. "Don't think this is over, Gael. I will see you defeated."

Diarmuid caught the contracts and tucked them inside his own tunic. "We'll have to see what Patrick de Cogan makes of the situation, but I fear you'll have enough to deal with explaining yourself to him." He gestured to the door. "Now that you've violated our hospitality, I have no hesitation in asking you to take your leave."

Harcourt gave Diarmuid a murderous look, strode to the door and left. A few moments later Maeve could hear hoofbeats retreating down the track, away from the tower house. She felt her breath release and turned to Diarmuid, resting a hand on his arm.

"Oh, I thank God you came when you did. I'm certain nothing good would have come if you hadn't."

He took her hand up in both of his and kissed it, drawing her into a brief embrace. She rested there in the comfort of his arms until he released her. He made his way over to Maeve's mother and led her to the fur covered chair.

"Find some rest in the chair here, lady mother. Maeve and I will attend to things up above."

"I thank you," she said, tears in her eyes. "Though I so

wanted Maeve to take the vows, I can say now that I am truly glad it didn't happen. I would be proud to call you my son."

"Thank you," he said and kissed the top of her head. "I could wish for no better wife, and no better mother-in-law."

He took Maeve's hand and led her up to the room above. He remained holding her hand and looked into her eyes. "I meant that. I promise I will do my best to honour and cherish you, Maeve, as I am bound to do, but also because it is my wish and desire to. I can only hope that someday you will care for me the way I have come to care for you."

Maeve looked deeply into his eyes, her heart filling with joy at his words. "Though we have known each other a short time only, I do care for you greatly," she said shyly.

Diarmuid put a finger to her lips. "Hush, I won't force you to say things that you cannot mean yet. Whereas you might have only known me a few days, Maeve, I have watched you and admired you from the first day I arrived at Teampall Gobnatan. I asked to be allowed to escort you here. I couldn't bear to think of anyone else with you as you faced the danger that the plague presented, though it might mean exile."

For a moment she was speechless. "We might still yet be stricken."

"I know," he said. "That's one reason I felt I had to let you know how I feel and I hope that my protection will be enough. It will suffice for Patrick de Cogan, I feel sure, but for the plague, we cannot know."

Maeve considered his words and realized that she could no sooner bear the thought of losing him to the plague or any other threat. She put a hand to his cheek and kissed his mouth. The kiss deepened, her lips becoming soft under his touch, her arms sliding around his neck, his arms supporting her. This was where she belonged. She knew that with a certainty that was rooted in the deepest part of her. They would face what was to come together, strong and determined. Surely that would please God.

Inspiration of Kristin Gleeson's The Blood of the Gaels

The inspiration for this story found its roots in my novel, *In Praise of the Bees*, set in sixth-century Ireland in the area of what is now Ballyvourney. The patron saint of the village is St Gobnait, who founded her community there in the sixth century. She kept bees and was widely known for healing with honey. I loved learning and creating as much as possible an authentic world of that time period in this rather removed area in Ireland where so much was in flux and always thought I would go back to it. When I was asked to write a piece for this anthology, it seemed like a perfect opportunity to do so. Though I set it later, during the time of the Black Death, it still features the places and the descendants of the original characters from the novel *In Praise of the Bees*.

Learn more about Kristin Gleeson at http://www.kristingleeson.com

The Heretic

By Lisa J. Yarde

Granada, Moorish Spain
June 1348

Ibn al-Khatib rapped on the door to the whitewashed residence of Granada's chief minister. Torches glowed on either side of the entryway, the crackle of the flames the sole sound. Although the wind had stilled, the fragrance of jasmine blooms lingered. Ibn al-Khatib contemplated the violet-hued beauty of the sky before he bowed his head. A small dark blotch on his gray silk tunic caught his gaze. Olive oil from the noonday meal! Why had he not noticed the stain beforehand?

The wood groaned before the door swung open in the grip of gnarled fingers, the tips dotted with red ink residue. The light of oil lamps set along the adjacent wall revealed a face with wizened features and deep crinkles beneath rheumy eyes. A gap-toothed smile beckoned.

Ibn al-Khatib bowed at the waist and straightened. "Honored master Ibn al-Jayyab. The peace of our God be upon you and your house forever."

With a grunt, the high minister inclined his grizzled head topped by a woolen cap. "And with you and yours always, Ibn al-Khatib."

As the master waved him in, Ibn al-Khatib entered and wiped the soles of his leather boots on a woven rug. "Where are your household servants?"

"Their intrusion is unnecessary." The olive-wood door thudded shut and Ibn al-Khatib glanced at his host, who continued, "Let us enjoy dinner in solitude. The bread is fresh. My cook made one of your favorite fish stews."

"God bless him and his hands. Lead on, master."

Despite Ibn al-Jayyab's rickety gait, Ibn al-Khatib followed him without comment from the antechamber through a lush garden courtyard. Rose and oleander bushes clustered around the central fountain. The companions sat side by side in the dining room on green silk cushions, washed their hands in a basin of heated rosewater, and dried them on linen squares. With a murmured blessing, Ibn al-Jayyab tore a large round flatbread and handed half to his guest. Steam wafted from platters of couscous cooked in a rich, golden broth, stuffed eggplants, liver sausages, saffron-scented lentils, and carrots coated in sesame paste, set alongside bowls of stewed shad fish. Ibn al-Khatib's stomach rumbled and he offered an apology.

His master chided in a rich baritone, "You've neglected your needs again."

Half-true, but Ibn al-Khatib bore too much respect for the man who had nurtured his career for over three decades to contradict him. "The sultan required my service. A page of the court brought me pickled olives in oil and pomegranate sherbet after the noon prayer."

"Then seven hours later, you've joined me at dinner. In your esteemed position as the sovereign's personal secretary, you may not disregard the master of Granada. But you should never forgo your needs, either. If a man does not aid himself, his neglect would always prove a greater distraction from his duties."

"Oh, my teacher, long years have passed since I sat at your feet and formed my first letters, but I am still learning from you."

"Indeed. Now eat."

The men feasted in near silence except for occasional sighs of delight and approval. Small bowls of syrupy-sweet fried bananas sprinkled with pistachios and carrot jam supplemented the meal Ibn al-Jayyab had offered. He nodded in consent as Ibn al-Khatib spooned moderate portions beside his bread.

Afterward, his host wiped his mouth with another cloth and leaned toward him. "I appreciate your company, although your family rarely sees you these days."

"They know about my devotion to my duties and to you, master. Without your influence, I would not have gained a role as the sultan's personal secretary."

"False modesty doesn't suit you. You've achieved by merit alone, but I expect more."

"I shall fulfill all of your desires for me and never disappoint you."

"You couldn't. I trust the members of your household are well, by the will of God?"

"Yes. My sons are dutiful. Their mother is a wise and patient woman, whom God blessed me to marry. Though I did not know it at the time." Then Ibn al-Khatib swallowed and cleared his throat. "I do not mean...."

Ibn al-Jayyab held up his gaunt hand, whereupon Ibn al-Khatib fell silent. "You need not apologize for the admiration you bear a much-beloved wife. It's no slight upon the offer, decades-old now, of my own exceptional daughter in marriage. She's content with her husband and children in Málaga."

"I'm pleased for her. Did our noble master mention the planned length of his absence? I dared not ask what he did not choose to reveal to me."

"He'll be gone for two weeks at most. He bid me remain rather than accompany him on this inspection of Málaga's fortifications. Though I suspect your friend Ibn al-Shaquri influenced the decision."

Ibn al-Khatib subdued a smile. "He is cautious in his new role as the sultan's chief doctor."

"Overly so. Why else would the physician recommend rest for a cold that lingered too long? As if I'm an old man upon my deathbed."

Ibn al-Khatib sipped cool water from a gilded goblet and kept silent about his mentor's advanced age of seventy-two years.

His host added, "The sultan's absence permits my

interest in another concern. I've had a second letter this morning from Ibn Khatima in Almería."

"Indeed." The base of the chalice in Ibn al-Khatib's grip hit the cedar tabletop with a heavy thud. His tight hold remained. "More news of this malady afflicting the poor there?"

"You should not dismiss their plight."

"I am merely uncertain of whether the sickness is great cause for concern as my learned colleague had previously implied."

"He's on hand in the city. You are not." Ibn al-Jayyab returned to the meal.

Chastened, Ibn al-Khatib joined him. "What does the good doctor say about the illness?"

"Thirteen deaths now in three weeks since his last letter. More sailors."

"The poor often suffer in their slovenliness and ignorance. They do deserve pity."

"They require proper care. Thus, your rival thinks nothing of aiding them."

"I have no rivalry with Ibn Khatima. I am more than ten years older than him. You once taught us both and we each excelled under your tutelage. He has gained great esteem as a medical doctor. Despite his obvious youth, his knowledge is admittedly advanced beyond mine. I do not begrudge him earned acclaim."

"Nor do you approve of his primary clientele."

Ibn al-Khatib sniffed. "A doctor aged twenty-four years with his supposed skill should show better discernment, or he will never find patrons among the elite families of Almería."

"A few of his rich patients make his generosity toward the less fortunate a worthwhile effort rather than a burden. Since when did you care about his prosperity?"

"A man must seek advancement or linger in the dust while his betters rise above him. I would hate to see Ibn Khatima fail."

"Then you'll have no objection to my request. The

reason I asked you to join me."

Ibn al-Khatib set aside the last spoonful of savory banana.

His master said, "Go to Ibn Khatima. Attend to him when he visits the poor, learn of their affliction, and report your findings. God willing, you shall discover his concerns are negligible."

"But, the sultan's new university—"

"I shall meet with the chief architect and builders in your absence. By the time you and our noble master have returned, my assessment will be ready. Complete this charge and you'll have my thanks. The sacrifice is minimal, a few days in the presence of Ibn Khatima."

"Master, I do not dislike him."

"But there is little appreciation for his methods. As he does not care about your... personal pursuits and interests —" When Ibn al-Khatib would have interjected, his master added, "Which we won't discuss further. I trust you above all others to verify these strange reports. At first, five deaths and hasty burials in the poor quarter of Almería did not perturb me much, except for the speed of the demise. Ascertain the truth. Are these deaths evidence of a virulent illness?"

Resigned, Ibn al-Khatib sighed. "God willing, I shall determine the possibility, my master."

Later he walked the dimly-lit corridors of his house, where his chief steward had greeted him with an oil lamp. A slave girl who swept the columned courtyard bowed and scurried out of his path. Then he mounted the wooden steps and entered a narrow doorway. He set down the oil lamp on a table, knelt between beds and regarded his sons, who slept soundly, unaware of the world's troubles.

Soon six years old in the middle of summer, Abdallah grew in the image of his mother. Ibn al-Khatib had named the boy for the grandfather he had never known, whose battlefield death had occurred in the service of the sultan eight years past, alongside Ibn al-Khatib's elder brother. God in His divine wisdom had made martyrs of such men.

He had also granted recompense with the births of Abdallah and his younger sibling, Muhammad. Ibn al-Khatib treasured his sons above all other persons, except one.

He rose and went into his bedchamber. Set the oil lamp in an empty wall bracket before he sank down on the mattress. No matter how many linens his wife had draped over the rough weft, the material pressed into the undersides of his thighs.

"If you again consider the disposal of our marital bed, I will continue my objections, dearest love."

He turned and reached for the slim shoulder across from him. "My Iqbal. I thought you might have been long asleep."

"How could I rest without my dearest love beside me?" Her husky tone filled the room. Then she rose and cast back the coverlet. Her shadow moved along the opposing wall as she went to another table between the lattice-covered windows, where an empty ceramic basin and ewer waited beside neat folds of cotton squares.

"We have slaves, lest you forget, my Iqbal. Why not call one of them? The redheaded girl or the one with her pockmarked face behind that damnable straw some might call hair?"

Iqbal's laughter pealed. "Such disdain!" She turned to him, cotton slung over her arm, the ewer gripped in one hand, and the basin atop the palm of the other. Pinpoints of light streaked through the windows. He sucked in his breath as silver beams illuminated the length of her legs beneath a wispy sleeping tunic. Thick coils of two black braids fell around narrow hips.

She added, "My dearest love, one day you might discover our servants have names if you took an interest." She chuckled again and approached him. "But tonight, they are of no concern. What care could slaves render that you might desire in place of the hands of your loving wife?"

When she reached him, he grasped the basin and set it on the carpeted wooden floor. At his feet, she knelt and removed his boots of Cordovan leather and woolen socks. He wiggled his toes while he admired the broad plain of her smooth brow and the fullness of lips he had kissed countless times since the birth of their eldest son. First with kindness and gratitude for the labor of a stranger turned companion. Passion and devotion had come, with a fervor he had never expected. Now, he must part from her.

"What are you contemplating?" She glanced up at him with those hooded brown eyes.

He bent and cupped her pointed chin, his pale hand in stark contrast against her dark flesh. "I can hide nothing from you. Nor would I wish to. I must leave for a short time."

Iqbal continued the fluid motion of trickling rosewater over his feet from ankles to soles until the liquid pooled in the basin. "I should have expected the noble sultan would need you."

"He does not. I am bound for Almería and a meeting with Ibn Khatima. There is a sickness in his city, which my master bids me investigate."

Iqbal dried his feet with the cloths. "Then you must do as the honored Ibn al-Jayyab asks."

She tossed the cotton into the ceramic bowl with the ewer and straightened. When she would have turned away, he jerked upright and caught her elbow.

"I won't shame myself again. No arguments with that arrogant wretch in Almería over religion. I promise." As she gazed up at him, he leaned closer. "You may believe me."

She dipped her chin. "I do." She went away and returned soon to his side. "If I must separate from you, my dearest love, then let us find joy in our marital bed."

He palmed the slightly raised roundness of her lower belly. By God's grace, another of their children would come at the start of winter.

"Are you certain?" He coughed and cleared his hoarsened throat. "That is, what has the midwife said of our relations?"

She regarded him. "You are always too good and gentle with me to harm our child."

He lifted her chin and peered deep into her eyes. "You did not ask the midwife after she last examined you. Muhammad arrived in such haste after we had...."

"I care not when I am in the arms of the man I love. My dearest husband."

He caressed her. To think, he had once sought the rich daughters of high court ministers and esteemed judges across Granada, only to find the true home of his heart with his Iqbal.

Almería, Moorish Spain
June 1348

"Seventy?" Ibn al-Khatib clapped a clammy hand to his forehead. "Seventy deaths now?"

"Lower your voice before you cause panic on the streets of Almería!"

Ibn al-Khatib's footsteps ceased. He stared in silence at his counterpart. Ibn Khatima's deep-set, ovoid eyes regarded him with mirrored intensity. They stood in the shadow of the upper city and the marble estates of its richest residents. Somehow, the young doctor had afforded a home here.

"Your daily visits to the poor quarter have not gone unnoticed, Ibn Khatima."

They eyed the city's occupants, whose cautious glances preceded hasty departures. Lightly veiled women in embroidered silk herded children before them, while their turbaned and bejeweled fathers and husbands rushed through the cobblestone streets. Some offered Ibn Khatima murmured greetings or tilts of their heads. But they watched Ibn al-Khatib with the same wariness as the sentries along the walls and at the city's westernmost gate had a day beforehand. Did they know death stalked the city?

The men fell into step beside each other. A casual observer might have thought of them as relations who favored one another in attire, height, and lean build. Even by the black sprigs of their neatly-trimmed beards.

Ibn al-Khatib adjusted the strap of his satchel and looked askance at Ibn Khatima. So reserved, unlike some men of his age. One of the youngest licensed physicians in the kingdom.

"You could have had a lucrative living, according to our honored master."

"I went where the people needed my services. Why did you study, Ibn al-Khatib? For the sake of pride and vanity? You have done better in life than me. I do not begrudge you any success. Must you question my choice?"

Ibn al-Khatib ground his teeth together. Insufferable wretch!

Then he cleared his throat. "We have quarreled once in public. I vowed never to make that mistake again. I have come at the behest of a man whom we both admire. In honor of him, let us put aside our differences."

"Agreed."

Ibn Khatima took a worn, cobbled alleyway and emerged into an even narrower street. Houses intermingled with cooking stalls, inns, warehouses, stables, and livestock pens. Even fewer people stirred outdoors than in the upper city. All manner of filth coated the trailing end of their light linen or cotton mantles, swept up from the muddied and filthy cobblestones.

The density of overhanging residences built on two floors allowed little light and air into the street below, an hour before midday prayers. Upon entry into the tanners' district, rank urine and the musty scent of hides permeated the air, but soon gave way to the brine of the Mediterranean Sea and the odor of rotten fish. A stout fishwife exited a thatched structure with a bloodied ceramic bowl of heads and eager cats clawing at her skirts. She clutched a fish head and raised her arm, but Ibn al-

Khatib's look made her draw back and stirred a chorus of mewls among the hungry animals.

"By the Prophet's beard!" he snapped. "The cure for most diseases may be found in sanitation. Not with blood and fish heads strewn across streets. Have you told these people?"

A long sigh followed. "We cannot interfere with the established practices of their livelihood. Would you deprive the cats, too?"

They turned left into an even narrower lane, emptied of all but the pair of learned men. The houses here, no more than rickety, wooden hovels, bore lime-wash marks on the doors. A wide, black streak marred other structures.

"The homes of the dead I have indicated with pitch. The rest are victims of the sickness who may have no hope," Ibn Khatima commented.

"Then whole families are affected?"

Ibn Khatima pointed to the nearest building with a crudely drawn pitch mark. "The father, a journeyman, died last night. First his eldest son, a sailor. Then two younger daughters. Afterward the mother, a rug seller who plied her trade near the docks."

They stopped at the last of the lime-washed houses. Ibn Khatima raised a gloved hand and knocked. A wide-eyed girl, possibly no more than five years of age, peeked out.

The scent of stale urine and unwashed bodies assaulted Ibn al-Khatib. He burrowed his nose in loose folds of the musk-scented turban while the girl gazed up.

Ibn Khatima said, "Peace be with you, little Amina. Do you remember me?"

"Doctor," she murmured.

"That's right. Are your parents still sick? May I come see them?"

As she withdrew, the litter of food scraps and grime on the floorboards came into view. The dankness and odor could have choked Ibn al-Khatib. Still, he managed a question.

"This child is the lone caretaker of her ailing parents?"

Ibn Khatima shrugged. "Not everyone can afford servants." Despite the scowl Ibn al-Khatib shot him, he went indoors and set his wooden box of implements, unguents, and medicines on the floor. He kept the leather satchel slung over his shoulder and withdrew behind a dilapidated curtain of hemp cloth.

Ibn al-Khatib stifled his nausea and entered the room though he stood apart from the girl. No apprehension or uncertainty reflected in the almond-shaped gaze she directed at him.

"Have you eaten, child?"

She shook her head and scattered golden-brown ringlets. He reached inside his bag and retrieved two of the four freshly picked apricots from the sole tree in Ibn Khatima's garden courtyard. He held the fruits out. She snatched them so fast, their fingers might have touched, but for the gloves.

"Learned Ibn al-Khatib, shall you join me, please?"

He answered Ibn Khatima's entreaty and cringed as the rough hemp scraped his sleeve. Behind the curtain, a couple lay prone on a pallet. Ibn al-Khatib could not restrain his gasp.

Two pustules the size of plums disfigured the woman's neck. The cadaverous man beside her had a blackened nose and fingertips. Perspiration poured from his hairline to his temple and his face had reddened, much like that of his bedmate.

Ibn Khatima had crouched beside the woman. "Amina, your sickness has advanced. Is there another who might care for the girl? What of your husband's family across the street?"

Her head lolled on the pallet. A tear trickled beneath crusted brown lashes. "Gone."

Ibn al-Khatib stepped back from the fetid odor of her breath, but his counterpart remained unmoved. "What do you mean, gone?"

"Left. Too afraid." She sucked in a ragged breath. "Water. So hot."

Ibn Khatima turned to the child, who finished the last of the apricots and tossed the seeds in the corner. "Little Amina. Are you fast and strong enough to fetch water?"

When she nodded with vigor, he commanded her to bring some. "In a clean cup."

Soon she returned. Ibn Khatima brought the vessel to his nose and sniffed before he addressed Ibn al-Khatib. "There is no contamination of the cistern in the sailors' quarter, which might account for this ailment."

He slid his gloved hand under the patient's head. Her lips, abraded and bloodless, latched on until liquid dribbled down her chin. Afterward, she crumpled on the pallet.

"Amina. My honored mother is a worthy woman. She could care for your child."

"No! My daughter is... she's all I have."

Ibn Khatima glanced at the little girl, who mopped sweat on the brows of her parents with a rag. Then the doctor shook his head, rose, and came around the foot of the pallet to the other patient. He lifted the ragged end of a dirtied shirt and exposed the jutting pelvic bone. Then he reached for the strings of the man's crinkled trousers at the waist without explanation.

Damnable man! To uncover a father before a child. Didn't Ibn Khatima maintain the modesty of his patients? He thought too well of himself and felt he need not enlighten anyone—

The outrage within Ibn al-Khatib's head and heart subsided as Ibn Khatima tugged aside the cloth and revealed an even larger boil, close to the man's groin.

"Do you understand, Ibn al-Khatib? These signs upon the neck, in the groins of men, the armpits of women. Then death claims them. Those who died first were all sailors on a ship out of Egypt, from Alexandria. The thirteen who followed, their wives and children. Rashid, their navigator, will join them soon. Do you see why I wrote in such haste to our honored master?"

Ibn al-Khatib could not repress a shudder. "Then the

reports from the Venetian and Genoese merchants at Málaga of nearly a year ago are true? The plague has reached our shores?"

"A new and virulent strain, unlike any I have ever witnessed. God, in His mercy, help us."

In the evening, Ibn al-Khatib paced the inner courtyard of his host's meager home. Meanwhile, Ibn Khatima stood beside the chipped edges of the fountain, where he tossed bread crumbs from their dinner to the sole, eager fish in the water.

"Read my notes. A scribe can create two copies, for you and our honorable master."

Ibn al-Khatib's footfalls ceased. "Can you afford the expense?"

Ibn Khatima's chuckle shook his slight frame. "You will have the sheaves of parchment before you depart in five days' time. Now, I shall study until the night prayer must occur. Join me if you wish. I've procured two chairs for the reading room, along with the writing desk, the stool, and the books. Despite my circumstances as you judge them."

"I meant no offense."

"I never suggested you offered it. I live well. Better than those poor people we saw today."

As Ibn Khatima proceeded into the tiny antechamber where he maintained a decent library, Ibn al-Khatib called out, "What will happen to the girl?"

"Her fate is inevitable. Did you think to change it with four apricots?"

Although Ibn al-Khatib had known the fruits would offer little sustenance, he had left them all. He sputtered, "But... but that cannot be! She's a child. You must do something."

Ibn Khatima looked over his shoulder. "It shall be as God ordains. Despite the divergence in our religious practices, we must agree that none of us may go against the will of God."

Granada, Moorish Spain
June 1348 – January 1349

"No, no, no! Ibn Khatima's conclusions are incorrect."

One week after his return from Almería, Ibn al-Khatib sat with his mentor beneath a shaded marble colonnade on the ground floor of Ibn al-Jayyab's residence. Two eunuchs on either side of them waved fans of thick palm leaves and cooled them. The cold glasses of blended pomegranate and lemon sherbet from which the ministers had sipped should have had the same effect. But Ibn al-Khatib discarded his rock-cut crystal glass on the table between them and tugged at the neckline of his tunic.

His mentor glanced at him. "What fault have you found with the doctor's observations?"

Ibn al-Khatib sneered before he rustled a sheaf of parchment. "He writes here, 'Believers, know the plague victim is a martyr. While Prophet Muhammad, may peace be upon him, warned not to go to a land attacked by the plague to avoid contagion, if any person resides or visits an area affected by the epidemic, he should not run away from the disease, since this condition is caused by God's will. Therefore, death is the Divine Decree and such misfortune is a testimony of martyrdom. You, who believe, know epidemics and plagues are the mercy of your Lord, the request of your Prophet, and the death of the pious who preceded you. Do not run away from them.' Nonsense! Would he have our people submit to the contagion?"

"Contagion?" Ibn al-Jayyab's shaggy eyebrows flared. "Have you concluded contagion afflicts Almería?"

"Honored master, with respect, how else may we explain the deaths of whole families? All those close to plague victims have suffered the effects and then died. There was a little girl...." Ibn al-Khatib paused and swallowed. "She showed the signs within a day of her father's demise. We could do nothing for her."

Ibn al-Jayyab patted his shoulder while he resisted an urge to shrug off the sympathetic gesture. Instead, he added, "Quarantine for sufferers could prevent contagion."

Then Ibn al-Jayyab removed his hand. "You might call down the wrath of Granada's clerics on your head. No Muslim can deny the will of God and avoid a fated death."

"You would have us surrender to the sickness?"

"The principal duty of our faith is submission before God. A herald arrived with word from the sultan. He shall enter the city this evening. On the morrow, we must request a private audience with him and reveal the sickness. You'll share Ibn Khatima's notes and your observations. Our noble master shall summon Ibn al-Shaquri and all other learned physicians of Granada to the council meeting. He will ask for recommendations. You'll remain silent. No mention of quarantine—"

"But, my teacher—"

"You have not garnered the experience which medical doctors have. Your theories cannot rival their actual practice. I forbid your interference. Besides, by the will of God, the plague may not spread beyond Almería."

Ibn al-Khatib flicked a glance at his mentor and then pressed his lips together. With a grunt, Ibn al-Jayyab rose and urged him to his feet.

"When my Abu'l-Qasim perished, my brilliant boy, my heart died too for a time. Then I grieved with you upon the demise of your own excellent father. We've long been a comfort to each other. More than a student and his tutor. Heed your foster father now, for you are the son I thought I had lost forever."

Ibn al-Khatib sighed. "I will always listen to you, my beloved master." He embraced the elder man, but in his heart, he already perceived the truth. The sickness they both feared would not remain in Almería.

Within two weeks, word of the plague spread as fast as the disease along the coast. In terror, Ibn al-Jayyab's daughter arrived with her entire family from Málaga at the height of summer's heat. Her father welcomed them, especially his grandchildren.

One evening after Ibn al-Khatib's sons and wife had

joined the chief minister's relatives for dinner, Ibn al-Jayyab withdrew into the spacious library and took his protégé with him.

"Where once there had been seventy deaths in one week, now there are at least seventy per day in Almería," the elder man pronounced as he read from a letter scribed in Ibn Khatima's handwriting. "The good doctor believes the disease may be managed. He has six recommendations listed. See here."

Ibn al-Khatib peered over his mentor's bowed shoulder. "True, fresh air by living in houses facing north and cool fragrances would do the poor some good. As would wheat and barley bread, hmm, yes, and lots of fresh water. But how can those who are surrounded by plague victims be as quiet as possible, have normal sleep, and normal bowel movements? I do not agree with bleeding either! It weakens people."

Ibn al-Jayyab chuckled and shook his head. "You must contradict Ibn Khatima at every opportunity. He's writing a treatise based on his early observations. I'll show Ibn al-Shaquri this letter on the morrow. Come, let's return to dinner. Your wife must wonder whether I've summoned you to work on the sultan's correspondence."

In the morning, the pair stood with Ibn al-Shaquri, one of the finest young doctors in Granada. His exalted position as the sultan's chief physician had not made him arrogant and he remained devoted to Ibn al-Khatib, who had guided his career in the manner of Ibn al-Jayyab.

Ibn al-Khatib said, "Do you not see matters as I do, Ibn al-Shaquri? Our noble master could close the gates of the cities and halt the spread of plague."

The younger man shook his head. "And ruin trade across Granada, my honored teacher?"

As a gasp filled Ibn al-Khatib's throat, the chief minister traded glances with both men, his lips quirked. "We cannot halt all commerce in the kingdom."

"Can the dead trade goods and coin?" Ibn al-Khatib threw up his hands. "A quarantine...."

38

He fell silent as his companions shook their heads. Ibn al-Jayyab turned and faced the opened window while Ibn al-Shaquri came to Ibn al-Khatib. "If this is the plague, it may abate in winter and cease altogether. We must have hope and faith. We cannot alter the will of God." He pitched his voice lower. "Fools and heretics would say otherwise."

The sultan and his family withdrew to their summer palace at the Generalife in the usual manner. Daily life in the capital continued with bi-weekly dispatches about the death tolls from varied coastal cities. By the time the sultan returned to Alhambra Palace, fewer reports arrived.

"It's just as I have said," Ibn al-Shaquri pronounced, while he and Ibn al-Khatib went to the chief minister's house. "The land is cooling. Plague does not thrive in cool climes."

Ibn al-Khatib made no reply, but he hoped winter would prove his friend right.

Before the first snows fell, Ibn al-Khatib and Iqbal stood alongside Ibn al-Jayyab while he shared poignant farewells with his family. Perhaps Málaga's suffering had come to an end for no deaths had occurred in recent weeks.

However, within days of the family's return, a letter from his daughter arrived for the chief minister, who summoned Ibn al-Khatib to his residence. While servants packed his belongings, Ibn al-Jayyab gave his steward instructions, and then spoke with Ibn al-Khatib.

"Honored master, I wish you would not go!"

"My youngest granddaughter has sickened and may have one parent left. I won't leave my daughter to suffer alone! Be dutiful and attentive to our noble sultan, but as I've reminded you, don't neglect your needs. Now embrace me as a son would his father."

Ibn al-Khatib hugged the elder man and kissed both his cheeks.

"By the Prophet's beard, would you squeeze the marrow from these old bones?" Ibn al-Jayyab drew back and cupped Ibn al-Khatib's chin. "Don't fear. Trust in God. If

He ordains my death, find comfort in the truth. No father could know the pride I have in you. The peace of God be with you always."

"And you, forever, my honored master."

"If your devoted wife should bear her son in my absence, send me word. I shall bless him upon my return."

A week later, the squalls of a newborn filled the birthing room of Ibn al-Khatib's house. After the midwife gave over his child, he called him Ali, the personal name of his mentor. One morning, the sultan demanded of him the whereabouts of Ibn al-Jayyab, who had returned to Granada two days beforehand and made no appearance at court.

"Noble master, I had not known of his homecoming! I'll seek him out at once."

But at Ibn al-Jayyab's house, the wild-eyed chief steward turned him away. "My apologies, minister, but my master will see no one today."

Ibn al-Khatib shot him a baleful stare but the eunuch's bulky form filled the doorway. "Not even me? Does some urgent concern occupy him? I can come again tomorrow."

"He will not see you then either, minister." The door closed with a heavy thud.

The next evening, with his duties completed, Ibn al-Khatib returned to his mentor's residence. A browbeaten eunuch, no more than twenty years of age, stood aside at his insistence. Indoors, Ibn al-Khatib wiped his feet and peered into the gloom of the house. No glowing oil lamps or their scent wafted from the kitchen.

He glared at the collared slave. "Take me to your master. Now."

At the top of the stairs to the family quarters, the chief steward rounded the balustrade. "Fool! I said, no visitors. Minister, you cannot go in to see the master! It's too dangerous."

A sudden chill swept over Ibn al-Khatib, but he mounted the steps. "Get out of my way!"

Despite his forcefulness, his fingers quivered when he

knocked at the door of Ibn al-Jayyab's chamber. "Honored master, I have come. May I enter?"

No answer. He regarded the chief steward, who shook his bulbous head. Wetness gathered beneath his eyes and he sniffled.

"Master! I will not leave until I have seen you," Ibn al-Khatib insisted. "Please, master. Let me attend you—"

"For mere moments, Ibn al-Khatib, and you will not move beyond the doorway."

He trembled at the subdued baritone echoing beyond the cedar. He gripped the handles and pushed inward.

The silvery glow of the moon illuminated the entrance to the room. Ibn al-Jayyab sat on a low stool along the wall beside a table, its surface almost obscured by a wide basin and ewer, two silver candlesticks, linens, and glass vials. The scent of incense, camphor and vinegar permeated the space.

Ibn al-Khatib's chest heaved as he looked upon his master, his foster father. Ibn al-Jayyab, unclothed from the waist up, lifted his spindly arm. With a dampened square of linen, he bathed the reddened area around an apple-sized pustule under his armpit.

"Strange. It no longer hurts," he whispered.

Ibn al-Khatib blinked back tears. "I'll summon Ibn al-Shaquri—"

"You will not."

"But, master—"

"No one else will die because of my folly. Especially that brilliant doctor with a bright future. You will leave this house of plague and never return. You'll tell our noble master of my fate and the danger in the capital."

With a sob, Ibn al-Khatib sank on the ground. "I can't abandon you!"

"You can. You must!" Ibn al-Jayyab lowered his arm. "Live, my son. You are all that is left of me in this world now. You will survive to fulfill my last request. A solemn duty. Ignore my earlier warnings. You were right. I was wrong. The pupil has bested the teacher. My greatest accomplishment at the hour of my death. Don't let accusations of heresy dissuade you. Speak to the sultan. Advise him about quarantine."

"How can I talk with him now, master? Father. Please...."

"It's too late for me but not the Moors of Granada. Go with God, my son. May He guide you. My blessings upon you until the end of time."

On wooden legs, Ibn al-Khatib stood, closed the door on his mentor forever, and staggered from the house. Tears blinded him, but he found his way home to his Iqbal. Alone in her presence, he knelt at her feet. She cradled his head against her belly as he wept.

Ibn al-Jayyab's funeral occurred three days after his death. At the sultan's command, Ibn al-Khatib had composed the elegy and delivered it beside the gravesite. The following morning, the sultan named him to Ibn al-Jayyab's post. Chief minister of Granada. The most powerful member of the council, his authority only superseded by the noble monarch.

Granada, Moorish Spain
October 1349

Ten months after his mentor's death, Ibn al-Khatib sat at his writing desk. Red ink stains dotted his hands. Sheaves of parchment in neat rows covered the table beside him.

"My dearest love, I thought you were coming after the evening prayer to bid your children goodnight. Yet, here you are."

He looked up and found his Iqbal in the doorway, the wet nurse behind her, and little Ali in her arms. He rose and came to them, pressed his lips to his tiny son's forehead.

Iqbal turned to the wet nurse. "Take him to the nursery and tell Abdallah and Muhammad their parents shall come and bless them shortly." Once alone, she glanced at her husband's writing area. "You still pursue this treatise. Your rebuttal to the words of Ibn Khatima."

He drew her to the high stool and sat her down. "I must complete the task. Not because he is wrong but, without this treatise, many more people will perish."

She shook her head. "You risk your career. The sultan heeded your recommendations for quarantine but charged you not to promulgate your theories about contagion...."

Iqbal trailed off as a knock at the door interrupted her. She bid the chief steward enter.

"Master. Mistress. A messenger from the kingdom of Morocco has arrived." The servant bowed and offered Ibn al-Khatib a roll of parchment, sealed with wax.

"At such a late hour?" He took the missive and opened it. Within moments, his heart thudded, and he gripped the wooden edge of the desk.

Iqbal stood. "My dearest love, what is it?"

"A letter from my sister in Taza. Our mother has died in that town. A plague victim."

"Oh, my dearest love. I grieve with you." Iqbal turned to the chief steward. "Give the messenger water and food."

When Ibn al-Khatib stood in solitude with her again, he gripped her shoulders. "My work must continue, even if in secret! Otherwise, these losses will have occurred in vain. My treasured mother. My honored teacher who was a father to me. Their deaths cannot be without consequence. Let others call me a heretic. God alone shall judge."

Salé, Morocco
September 1361

In the coolness of an early morning, Ibn al-Khatib sat on a wooden bench atop the stone roof of his house. The wide vista offered a view of the harbor at Salé, dotted with the ships of Moroccan fishermen, merchants, and pirates.

Although the kingdom's ruler had granted him this temporary residence north of the capital at Fez almost a year beforehand, Ibn al-Khatib still marveled at the sights. Far from his homeland.

"You wonder if we'll ever return to Granada, my dearest love?"

Iqbal's slim hand alighted on his shoulder. He drew her beside him. As she sank down, a low groan escaped her. She pressed her brow against his temple.

"You should not have exerted yourself on the steep stairs. A slave could have called me."

"I missed you." She glanced at the prayer rug rolled up at his feet and the almost empty basin. "You made your ablution and performed the dawn prayer alone?"

"Our sons were with me. They stored their rugs afterward."

Her husky laugh followed. "And returned to bed. I looked in on each of them. At least none of our female servants occupies Abdallah's bed."

"Not that you saw. He has the desires of a man aged nineteen years. I shall seek out a suitable marriage to temper those passions."

"Did you speak with our noble master about your intent when he visited in the spring?"

"I shall approach the Moroccan ruler instead, in Fez."

"Then you don't believe in our young master's plans for recapturing the throne of Granada?" Iqbal raised her head. "This exile has already lasted three years. We will leave."

"Our noble master is not his father, but rather a young man of twenty-three years, robbed of his kingdom and forced to seek sanctuary here. The request for aid he bade me write in the spring to the king of Castile has gone unanswered. For now, our lives are here, my Iqbal."

She leaned against him once more while he turned and nuzzled her brow, etched with faint lines. "How do you fare today?"

She cleared her throat. "Better. I'll visit the marketplace. I've been mired in this house for weeks now. All because of a cold."

"You forget the fever, which accompanied your illness." He ran his fingertips along the bone-dry skin stretched across her hands. "Stay with me."

"Don't coddle me like I do our little Ali, my dearest love."

"Never. But I have missed you at my side during the day."

Her laughter pealed, but soon subsided in a coughing fit. He rubbed her back until she quieted. "Stay."

"You won't even realize once I'm gone. Our children have told me of your long hours spent in the writing room. Still working on that treatise?" She drew back and frowned at him. "Isn't it enough that your rivals in Granada have questioned your adherence to Sufi doctrine?"

"My Iqbal, Sufis are no less devout than other Muslims. As for the treatise, the plague followed us here last year and devastated Fez in the summer until the pestilence abated. With each occurrence throughout these thirteen years, I've learned as much about this disease as Ibn Khatima and Ibn al-Shaquri. Surely, you see why I must continue to document its effects and suggest possible treatment methods?"

She looked away, but he grasped her chin. When their gazes met, she sighed and nodded. "You have enemies. They've long sought to eliminate your influence, first over the former sultan and now his son."

"I don't fear those jealous fools. Only the loss of your indulgence."

She placed a light peck on his cheek. "You have my heart. I have yours. How could you ever lose my support?"

As Iqbal had predicted, he adjourned to his writing room during her absence, until she found him later. Then they dined with their sons.

"I wish you might remain a little longer with us." Iqbal reached for the hand of their youngest boy across the low table.

Ali said, "Mother, I'm almost thirteen years old now.

Attendance at the University of Al-Quaraouiyine in Fez is a great honor. It's the oldest school in the Islamic lands."

"He'll be well. I'll look after him as I've done with Muhammad," Abdallah promised.

Their father smiled. "Three fine scholars. What more could we ask for, my Iqbal?"

He stretched out beside her early that night after prayer. He sought her fingers beneath the cotton coverlet. "I miss our old bed in Granada."

When she giggled, he hushed her. "What will our slaves think?"

She turned her head on the pillow and pressed her brow against him. "You don't care if they hear me laughing abed."

"You're warm again tonight."

"It's just hot in the room."

But in the morning, the fevered sensation had worsened. Iqbal had perspired most of the night and tossed aside the cover. Listless, she barely roused herself for the dawn prayer.

"My Iqbal, rest. I'll send a slave to fetch the doctor."

She sagged on the bed and gave a barely perceptible nod. "Hurry."

The physician came and went. Then on the third day after her visit to the marketplace, at noon, Iqbal complained of chills. Ibn al-Khatib sent for the doctor once more. She coughed and sweated during his examination.

"As her husband, you should not remain in close proximity while she's sick."

"I'm not abandoning my Iqbal! Not until I know her ailment. If you can't determine a cause and cure, I'll find someone else who can. Take your coins and go!"

Later, Abdallah pleaded, "Father, even if this is the return of a bad cold, you shouldn't stay beside Mother. Please. The room across the hall is empty, with Ali and Muhammad's departures. I can't delay and must resume my lessons in Fez, too. But I'd fare better on the journey if I knew you would take precautions."

Ibn al-Khatib waved him away. At night, he entered the abandoned chamber of his younger sons. He remained awake long after stars glittered in the sapphire sky.

Stillness had settled over the house. Iqbal's coughs no longer echoed. He crossed the room, flung open the door, and stepped into the darkened hallway. His palm flattened against the entrance to the bedchamber he shared with his wife, he pushed inside.

Dim candlelight revealed how her chest still rose and fell with every ragged breath. A low cry filled his throat. He approached but remembered Abdallah's entreaty.

He whispered into the gloom. "Don't leave me."

Fingers of first light crept over the land while he sat in his writing room and pored over the treatise. He scrubbed a hand over his burning eyes and only looked up when Abdallah knocked.

"Father, Mother's chief attendant says you must come!"

Both men rushed upstairs. The servant sobbed at the opened doorway of Ibn al-Khatib's quarters. Inside, Iqbal lolled on the pillow, her brow coated in perspiration. Hair clung to her temple. When she groaned and turned her face toward the pinpricks of illumination streaming through the lattice-covered window, her thick curls fell away. A reddened pustule, no bigger than a grape, dotted her neck.

"No!" Ibn al-Khatib rushed forward, but his son restrained him.

Abdallah sobbed. "Father, please."

"She can't die!"

Ibn al-Khatib wrenched free and ran down the steps. Despite tears, he scoured copious notes and letters exchanged with doctors in Granada over the years, including Ibn Khatima and Ibn al-Shaquri. They knew of persons who had lived, sole survivors robbed of the rest of their families by plague.

"Father." Abdallah had followed him. "You must quarantine yourself, too."

"Yes, yes! Do the same for a week until we are sure you are not affected. I'll help your mother. I won't stop until

I've saved her. Now, where was that last letter from Ibn al-Shaquri?" He soon found the dated correspondence. "Ah! The tip of a hen feather may be inserted into the boil and then drainage will occur."

At Abdallah's gasp, he promised, "I'll wear gloves! I'll be cautious."

He returned to the shared chamber. The door would not budge, even when he shouldered it.

He called out, "My Iqbal? Why have you latched the door? My Iqbal! Answer me."

A groan preceded her soft voice. "I love you...." Then utter quiet followed.

Granada, Moorish Spain
December 1362

Winter's chill settled over Granada and seeped through the shuttered windows. In his old house, Ibn al-Khatib set down a missive from his eldest son. Abdallah promised the brothers lived well, safe from plague in Fez. Their father missed them and their mother, too.

Once the young sultan had reclaimed his throne seven months after Iqbal's death, he had appointed Ibn al-Khatib as chief minister, and he resumed his duties.

The nights offered solitude. After every evening prayer and his meal, he sat at his writing desk. An ink-stained reed in hand, he scribbled upon the pages of his treatise about the plague. For fourteen years, the disease had dominated his life. Robbed him of his mother and foster father. His Iqbal. The young sultan knew of his theories about contagion and quarantine, abhorred them as much as the Sufi doctrines Ibn al-Khatib espoused. But for the sake of his long service, he enjoyed protection from his enemies. What could they do to him now? What more did he have to lose?

Inspiration of Lisa J. Yarde's The Heretic

In the summer of 1374, rivals of the Granadan high minister Ibn al-Khatib sent men to strangle him in a Moroccan jail. After burial, his attackers exhumed his body and burnt it. His remains are interred in the Bab al-Mahruq cemetery in Fez. Until his demise, Ibn al-Khatib had spent the last months of his life in self-imposed exile from Granada, accused of various crimes, including treason and religious heresy. His enemies had called for the confiscation of his property and burnt his works in the Moorish capital's market square four years prior to his death. His opinion on the causes and treatment of the Black Death survives in his treatise begun between 1349 and 1352.

Ibn al-Khatib made no mention of the impact of his personal losses resulting from the plague. Custom did not invite Moorish medieval writers to include the details of their lives in their writings. The only sources of reference are the elegies he composed after the deaths of his mentor Ibn al-Jayyab and his wife Iqbal. While the loss of his mother occurred due to plague and the other deaths happened during verified instances in Spain and Morocco, some historians dispute the death of Ibn al-Jayyab from the disease. There is also no specific cause listed in the sources for Iqbal's sudden death, which purportedly occurred on September 7, 1361.

On the names and depictions of historical figures, I opted for the patronymic rather than personal names of the male characters. In Arabic, Ibn means "the son of" hence Ibn al-Khatib, or "the son of the preacher." The name Iqbal means "luck" in Persian, but it's uncertain whether Ibn al-Khatib would have first found the term apt in his search for a wife. His characterization as something of a social climber derives from several sources, especially *The Great Ruling Families of the Fourteenth Century:*

Muṣāhara in the Age of Ibn al-Khaṭīb by Dr. Josef Ženka, which mentions the minister's earlier contrivance to marry into the most prominent families in fourteenth-century Granada. His rivalry with Ibn Khatima was complex but based upon Ibn al-Khatib's adherence to Sufi doctrines, which orthodox Islam rejected. Of the relationship between Ibn al-Jayyab and Ibn al-Khatib, the historian M. J. Rubiera has described it as "... the mutual spiritual adoption of a father for a son; the master even coming to promise his own daughter in marriage to his disciple, as was common in many cases, even if the union did not come to fruition...."

Ibn al-Khatib inherited his mentor's powerful role in Granada, but remained as helpless against the adversaries who derailed his career as he did while the Black Death ravaged Europe in the Middle Ages. The idea of transmission of disease through contagion would remain unaccepted in the Islamic world until the nineteenth century.

Learn more about Lisa J. Yarde at http://www.lisajyarde.com

50

Little Bird

By Laura Morelli

Siena, Italy
1348

"Lift your skirt, girl."

With the tip of his walking stick, Zio prods the ragged hem of my shift, where the ruddy earth has caked around the stitching.

"Go on."

From the edges of the vegetable stalls, a few market-goers turn to look at us, wide-eyed and fidgeting.

Zio—he's not my *real* uncle, nor anyone else's as far as I know, though everyone calls him Zio and he's as much family as I might ever claim—raps the tip of his gnarled cane on the cobbles. The noise captures the attention of a few more women, who have stopped looking at the wheels of cheese, and have turned in our direction.

"She was born in Salerno," Zio's story begins without preamble. He paces before a pile of ham hocks covered in bristles, his voice echoing in the *campo*, "...the daughter of the apothecary where I was an apprentice. Her mother went to the World to Come as the child came forth. But from birth, *signore e signori*, she was marked. Marked by the Enemy." He pauses. I hear a woman's gasp.

At the edge of the nearest stall, Elia, the old woman who travels with us, has set up her wheeled cart with its assortment of glass vials and crushed powders wrapped in tiny scraps of sackcloth. As Zio comes to the end of his speech, she will unfurl the tarp to display our wares, and she will remove the linen hood that hides her colorless hair, her nearly transparent skin, and her pale, pink-rimmed eyes.

The sun glows around the edges of the rooftops, casting Siena's tower as a long, skinny shadow across the square. The market overflows with cabbages, beans, and cheeses. Vibrant flags flap from the stone window ledges, and fine horses are hitched to iron rings. In spite of the heat, women browse the market stalls wearing heavy brocades that hiss over the cobbles, their hair adorned with tortoiseshell and ribbons.

A wealthy town.

Zio's hooded eyes are barely visible above the wiry, chestnut beard that conceals so much of his face that it is hard to know what he is thinking. Still, I know he senses that we might do well here.

"Now I shall tell you how this child became marked in this most unusual way," he continues. That's the beginning of the next part, a tale I've heard so many times I could recite it myself.

Skirting along the edge of the onlookers, a girl appears. She is around my own age, I think, with hair the color of fire. She holds the hand of a younger version of herself— her sister?—so the two do not become separated. For a moment, I wonder what it must be like to be raised in a town like Siena, with its looming towers, its slick horses, its well-fed women.

I feel Zio's cane at my feet again, and I crunch the rough fibers of my shift in my fists. The hem rises from the stones.

"Her feet!" I hear an older woman whisper. She presses her elbow into another woman beside her. "Look." A few people in the back of the crowd strain to see over the shoulders of those in front. The red-haired girls turn toward us.

"No doubt you have noted the wounds," Zio says. "You see, then, what I saw in this orphan child. I knew that the concoctions I learned to make in her father's shop could help her, could help others who suffer strange symptoms. But there is more to the story, *signore e signori.*"

These words are my cue to release my skirt and raise my hands, displaying my palms to the crowd. A single gasp rises from the collective murmur.

From the back of the crowd, a woman shrieks.

"Stigmata!"

It is always better if one of the townspeople cries out the word. If we have done our job well, we never have to say "stigmata" ourselves. That's what Zio tells us, as we sit in the fire's glow in a field outside of town, sharing a morsel of food that Paolo has collected through means either honest or debatable. We do not ask.

"Be still, Little Bird."

Zio drags a piece of cut glass over the scabs and thickly scarred skin that have formed over the last gash. A dark trickle of blood spurts from the center of my palm. I do not turn away. Tomorrow morning, before we amble up the steep paths of the rock to the city gates, I will rub more red pigment into the wound.

He is clever, my *zio*, I think. Experienced in the skills of our trade.

Elia is the one who named me, after my skinny arms and legs, which she has tried in vain to fatten. She stretches out in the shadows of the wagon, visible only as a wraith of white among our sackcloth, bundles of linen, and wooden boxes containing our precious ingredients. She will tuck me in next to her warm body before going to sleep, to make sure the men don't get any ideas, she says. From the wagon's tailboard, Paolo watches the landscape go dim from under the brim of his cap, as shards of whittled wood fall away between his dangling legs. Our crooked mule stands silent, one leg cocked. The spire of Siena looms over us like a ship's mast.

In the distance, I watch the city gate creak open. Three men haul a cart down the slope of the hillside, staggering under its weight.

"Why don't we stay inside the walls?" I blurt. "It's safer and more beautiful there. Inside."

Zio lifts the shard of glass from my palm. I see his eyes flash in the glow of the firelight, then he lets out a small puff of a laugh. "What do you speak of, Little Bird?"

I hesitate. "We are always out here. Away from the people."

Zio nods. "You know they do not want us inside."

I know he is right, but I still desire to look into their windows. I do it in every town. Blacksmiths. Weavers. Goldsmiths. Makers of belts, beads, bread. Peering into the cracks and open windows at dusk, I see men and women toiling, whispering, laughing with their families and neighbors. I see parents around tables, children piled three, four, five to a bed, bound together against the cold and rain.

I hold no hope of being one of them, one of those who lives an ordinary town life.

I turn away from my bleeding hand and give my attention to the distance, to the giant hewn stones that make up the walls of Siena. A new moon rises, framing the spiky silhouette of cedars. To the west, heavy, foreboding clouds have gathered and the air turns still.

A town of rich merchants, Elia has said. A town wealthier than Salerno, even Pisa, that stinking hole of a port. In Pisa's market square, they grew suspicious right away. Wary of us. Distrustful even of me, a mere girl. When that happens, it is time to move on.

We bring to town our wounds, our strangeness, for all to see. All of us, that is, except for Paolo. His wounds are on the inside; at least that's what Elia says. Paolo would never say such a thing. He doesn't talk much. He's the only one of us who can get a respectable job. In Siena, the joiner's guild didn't hesitate to hire him as a day laborer. It seems they need a lot of help in the cathedral work yard, and he is the only one of us who might pass for an ordinary person.

"Maybe they wouldn't be so suspicious of us if we stayed inside the city with them."

This time it is Paolo who silences me, glancing over his shoulder from the tailboard of the cart.

"You don't want to stay in there, Little Bird," he says, pulling the brim of his hat lower over his forehead. "Many sick people. Some try to bring them into the cathedral while I am working. Better out here. Zio is correct."

I watch the men with the heavy cart lumber out to an open place beyond the walls, where someone has dug a fresh pit. They tip their cargo into the pit, then they light a fire, their distant voices carried up into the dusk along with curls of smoke.

A shiver crackles up my spine like the legs of a spider. It reaches into my gut, long before I register the acrid stench in my nostrils.

Death.

I look at my palm now, my old scars freshly opened.

"Good," Zio says. He sets down the piece of broken glass on a rock, then walks out to survey the men with the cart as the night envelops us.

The distant men rattle the empty cart back through the gates of Siena, which close behind them with a great creak and a clatter of metal. The gates will reopen for us when the sun rises.

The red-haired girl is back.

This time she is leading a man by the hand, wending her way through the market toward Elia's cart.

"No doubt you have noted the wounds, *signore*," Zio is saying to a new group of women who have gathered to examine my palms. "You see, then, what I saw in this orphan child. I knew that the divine nature of God had revealed himself in this simple girl. And that the concoctions I learned to make in her father's shop could help her, could help many other people who suffer."

Beside Elia's cart, the red-haired girl picks up one of our small linen bags and turns it over in her hand. She loosens the string and smells the powder inside. Then she hands it to the man to examine.

Zio continues. "As I have told you, my esteemed friends, I learned from the most illustrious apothecary of Salerno. I have relieved thousands of people of their suffering. And I can help you, too!"

What the Sienese don't know yet is that I, the girl with the demon's marks turned into stigmata, am just the beginning. Over the coming days, Zio will demonstrate how Elia can heal just by laying her alabaster-white hands on the sick, how he has brought Paolo back from the brink of death, and how he can help others, too, with everything from moles to toothaches, baldness, even diarrhea.

After we've sold our elixirs, we will return to the countryside. Elia and I will capture snails, eating the meat and grinding the shells. We will gather mushrooms, plants, and stems. We will trade with others on the way. We will grind powders and sew together tiny bags of linen and sackcloth to contain them.

Now that the Sienese have understood the point of our little demonstration, many people have turned their backs and returned to the market stalls. No doubt we are not the first such hawkers in their squares.

But Zio is not worried; I know that. It is only our second day in Siena. He won't convince everyone this time, but we will sell something. Meanwhile, Paolo is paid a little money as a laborer. In the evening, we will hand what we earned over to Zio, and he will make sure we eat. Before long, if we have done our job well, the townspeople will have bought our stock. And after a few weeks or months, before anyone returns to complain, we will have packed up our wagon and moved on to the next town.

This time, though, it doesn't take weeks or months before someone speaks against us.

"You're a fake!" A voice hisses, snake-like, from the pork seller's table. A brawny woman steps out from behind the stall. "Why are you listening?" She brandishes a dirty rag, waving it at the small group huddled around Elia's box of cures. "Are you dull?" She points a pudgy finger to her head. "They will only take your money, and what will you have to show for it?" She challenges the few potential customers before turning on Zio himself.

"And you..." she begins. "You and your unnatural friends are not welcome here. We will not be taken advantage of so easily." She crosses her broad arms.

"*Signora*," Zio says, bowing toward her as if she were a noble lady, "forgive me if I have given you an inaccurate impression. I can see that you are a woman whose fairness is matched only by her intelligence..."

The woman continues to cross her arms, but her scowling lips waver. I know how this part goes, too, so I turn my attention to the girl examining our powders. She has convinced Elia to let her pour a small bit of powder into her palm. I recognize it immediately. Elia and I have experimented with mixing the blood of the insects clinging to the oak trees, along with powdered seashells we collected near Pisa. A striking shade of red.

"Look, papa," the girl says, opening her palm. "Is this not the color?" Her father runs his fingers across his daughter's outstretched palm, then lowers his long nose into the powder, his disheveled black hair falling around the collar of his paint-stained shift.

"I ground it myself," I tell them, approaching the box.

"What's in it?" the man turns his brown eyes on me.

I hesitate. We are not supposed to reveal our ingredients.

"Our own custom mixture, *signore*," Elia says, setting her colorless eyes on the man. "The cure is effective against boils. I would be pleased to advise you on its use."

"Thank you, but I'm as healthy as a horse," he chuckles, patting his paunch. "At least I have no boils. But I shall pay you for a bag or two of the powder all the same. For painting."

A painter. I should have known, looking at the state of his linens.

"Very well," Elia says, knowing better than to argue with

a paying customer, even if he will find his own use for the powder. She extends a chalky palm to receive his coins.

"You will use it for color?" I ask. The red-haired girl turns her freckled face toward me.

"Pigment," the girl answers. "I am a grinder, too," she says. "I mix pigments for my papa. He is one of the most important painters in Siena." I see her chest inflate. "Lorenzetti. Surely you have heard of our workshop."

I have no reason to have heard of these Lorenzetti, but something about the girl's demeanor makes me feel ashamed for not knowing.

Before I have a chance to formulate an awkward answer, a ragged man scrambles into the square, nearly out of breath.

"*Dottore*! Help!" His eyes scan the crowd, then land on Zio. "Please! You have a remedy for pestilence?"

"Pestilence?!" the fat pork-seller finally stops her tirade against Zio and turns toward the hysterical man.

"My neighbor and his wife... They broke out in sores three days ago. And it is now spreading on our street. Five more today in the *contrada* of Valdimontone. God help us!"

"Come, sir." Zio slips out from under the searing gaze of the pork-seller and leads the man by the arm to Elia's cart. "Let us help you."

I watch the red-haired girl and her painter father retreat from the square. Suddenly, I am seized with a strange fear that they will disappear into the fabric of the city and I will never see them again. Checking to make sure Zio and Elia are not watching, I follow the pair out of the sun-filled *campo* and into the shadows of a narrow alley.

The painter's daughter does not know that I have been following her.

The truth is that I've been trailing her for days, stealing away from Zio and Elia in the square, hanging back so that she does not sense me behind her shoulder. I duck into the doorways of fine houses, the porticos of the city's churches, watching her dark red head bob through the clusters of people in the squares and market halls.

The painter's daughter pulls her younger sister, a smaller version of herself, by the hand. Together they cut a circuitous path through the more crowded areas of town, avoiding the *contrade* of Drago, Oca, and Brucco, where wooden barriers have been erected at the entrances to the streets, wooden crosses are nailed over the doors, and carts leave the quarters by the hour with bodies stacked three and four deep.

The pestilence has crept around the edges of the city, pushing people into the center, but the *contrada* where the painter's workshop lies remains full of life. Here, residents have begun to unfurl colorful flags from their window ledges and are erecting long wooden tables down the middle of the streets in advance of some kind of festival.

The Lorenzetti workshop carries a particular aroma that wafts into the alley long before you reach it. The smell is acrid but not unpleasant, a mixture of vinegar and the hearth. I haven't yet gathered my nerve to peer into a crack in the half-open shutters.

"Would you like to come inside?"

A deep voice crackles in my ear. I catch my breath in my chest.

The painter.

I recognize his lean figure, the long, black hair swept away from his face, the thick beard flecked with silver. He must have been walking in the street, not far behind me. Heat flashes across my cheeks.

"The girl with the stigmata, if I am not mistaken?"

His brown eyes are soft and kind, almost laughing, but I cannot bring myself to meet his gaze. I am full of shame that he has caught me trying to peer into his workshop window.

"I... I wondered if you might like more red pigment, *signore*." I study my bare toes and red-smudged feet, which protrude from the bottom of my dirty shift.

"Come in," he says. He presses the wooden door and gestures for me to step over the threshold.

I hesitate.

"Please."

One step into the cool dimness of the Lorenzetti studio, and I am overcome. The room is filled with large wooden panels in different states of preparation. On a worktable in the center of the room, a great battened panel glistens with fresh gilding. Another man sits before a smaller panel, working in intense concentration with a fine brush. Beyond the workshop, I glimpse the kitchen, where the girls have joined a plump woman rolling out dough.

Along the back wall, glass jars filled with colored powders clutter the shelves. Signor Lorenzetti presses his hands on a table littered with colored dust, and marble mortars and pestles.

"Surely this is a familiar sight to you?" Lorenzetti gestures to the jars of pigment.

I barely find my voice. "No, I admit that have never seen such a thing, *signore*."

"My daughters grind most of the pigments for my brother and me, but sometimes we procure special pigments from elsewhere." His eyes remain soft, unthreatening.

"Something cool to drink, *cara*?" The plump woman emerges from the kitchen, followed by the painter's daughters.

The older girl follows me with her brown eyes, nearly the same as her father's but more piercing, less friendly. Have I underestimated her? Has she understood that I have been trailing her?

"This doesn't look familiar?" She gestures to the pigments. "I thought you were raised in an apothecary in Salerno. I heard the powder seller say so."

"Were you?" the younger sister asks. The tiny girl's eyes are even more searing, blacker.

Was I?

The question hangs heavy and unanswered in the air.

I had always assumed so, but for the first time I realize that I have no memory of any of it—of the apothecary shop, of Salerno, of my own parents.

Master Lorenzetti heaves himself onto a wooden stool and slices through the thick atmosphere with a conciliatory tone. "If you would be so kind as to procure us some more crimson pigment, *signorina*, from your..."

"My uncle."

He nods. "Your... *zio*. Yes. I would be most grateful."

"I can get it for you," I say quickly. My heart beats wildly in my chest. How will I ferret it away without Elia or Zio noticing? I don't know.

"*Bene*. Then it is agreed. We will pay a fair price. We have our color-sellers here in Siena, of course, but it is not like Venice, where you can buy rare pigments all day long. I understand that your *zio* is selling cures, not pigments. But when we find something unique, we must avail ourselves of the opportunity no matter what the source, no?"

Then the artist reaches for my hand and opens the palm, drawing it close to him. I feel his sure grip, the slightly rough texture of his fingertips. With his index finger, he traces a line of rough scab down the middle of my palm. He looks closely at the red pigment pressed into the wound, the same as the pigment he has bought from us. Then meets my eyes.

"Your... *zio*," he says. "He cares for you?"

"Of course," I say, drawing my hand away and tucking it away into the fold of my shift. "He has always provided."

"But your marks..." he says. "Those were not really made by divine intervention, I suspect?"

I feel my mouth open but no words come out. No one has ever questioned my wounds, not even looked at them that closely.

Then I see the skin next to the painter's eyes wrinkle again, teasing me without words. He lowers his voice to a whisper as if trying to keep a secret from the others in the workshop. "You see, *signorina*? I have daughters. I am wise to the games of girls."

He wags a bony finger at me in a playful scold. "It's alright. Your secret is safe within these walls, as long as we can count on you to bring us more of that pigment."

In a field beyond the city walls, the grave pits have widened. At dusk, laborers heave carts laden with the dead out of the city gates. The wrapped bodies are stacked higher with each passing day, layers upon layers of the stricken.

Zio and I move from square to square, but after only a few weeks, the main *campo* of Siena counts more penitents than market-goers. Lines of men, and even women, beat their backs bloody with long, knotted ropes. They intone chants that haunt my dreams. Have the Sienese sinned so deeply that they have brought this punishment on themselves? The question is on everyone's lips, looming large and unanswered.

We have urged our mule to carry the wagon farther out onto the plain, still within view of Siena's watchtowers and imposing walls, but far upwind from the pits and the fires where the clothes and goods of the dead are heaved into the flames. From under an oak tree, Zio watches the city warily, adjusting the leather straps of the money purse he keeps pressed against his chest.

Paolo and I sit side by side, our legs swinging off the back of the cart, he with his ever-present hat and whittling knife, I with my mortar and pestle. Elia has spent the day gathering olives and plants in her aprons, and snitching apricots from a nearby farm. She appears like a ghost at the edge of a grove of trees, a surreal vision that still has the power to startle me when I least expect it.

I have collected several scaly insects from the branches of the oak tree, dropping their crusty bodies into a jar of vinegar. I have also tucked a bag of ground murex shells from our stores in the wagon into my pocket, so that I can prepare more pigment for Signor Lorenzetti. I hope he will be pleased. Over the past weeks, I have collected coins in my own small purse. It's the first money I have ever earned for myself, without handing it over to Zio. I have not told anyone that I am selling pigments to the painter. For the first time in my life, I feel something like exhilaration.

"Paolo," I say, my voice lowered. "Do you remember when Zio left Salerno with me? When I was a baby?"

He shakes his head. "I only met Zio and Elia later, in Naples, when they let me join them. You were a big girl by then."

"You never knew anything of my family? My father? The apothecary shop?"

He shakes his head again.

"Do you believe him? About where I came from, I mean?"

Paolo stops whittling and meets my gaze. "Why wouldn't I?"

I am silent. I do not have any way to know, do I?

Paolo shrugs. "What difference does it make now, Little Bird? Does he not take care of us?"

"Does he?" We sit in silence, then Paolo returns to running his dull knife over a smooth piece of olive wood. I wish I had an answer, or could make myself not care like Paolo, but the question nags at me. I wonder what name my parents might have given me. It probably was not Little Bird.

I know that Paolo has handed over the money he has made to Zio, everything he has ever earned as a day laborer. All of us eat thanks to Paolo's more legitimate line of work, yet he carries no purse of his own.

"Where are you, Little Bird?" Zio's grumbling voice rises. I hide my red-stained mortar and pestle behind the small of my back as he hobbles around the side of the cart.

"There is a horse race; I have heard of it in the market," he says. "We must be prepared. There will be customers. Let us refresh your marks. Then you will help Elia with the posies."

Reluctantly, I follow Zio around the other side of the cart, where Elia is tying small bouquets of dried oregano, eucalyptus, and lavender flowers, and tossing them into a large basket. We have sold them in Pisa and Lucca, where the ladies pressed them to their noses while they walked the streets. The posies are effective at warding off the plague vapors, at least that is what Zio tells his customers.

"She has made herself scarce," Elia says.

"Where have you been, Little Bird?" Zio flicks his hooded eyes at me.

"I have been collecting food," I say. "And looking for opportunities, as you say we must." I gather my nerve. "Zio. Have you considered that we might stay here in Siena, at least through the winter?"

He pauses, then barks out a loud laugh. "What on earth for?"

"Because... I think we could do well here. Siena is a rich city, you have said so yourself. And the people... They are willing to pay for things, *real* things, like pigments, that we could sell without having to put on a show in the square. We could set up a shop. We could be pigment-sellers. Apothecaries."

Zio and Elia exchange a fleeting glance that I fail to interpret. Zio's mouth turns into a thin line, but Elia jumps in. "Why would the guilds approve a group of vagabonds like us in their midst? That will never happen as long as we live, child."

"Correct," says Zio. "Besides, have you not seen the God-forsaken coming out of those gates every day?" He gestures to the city walls. "This Great Mortality will only get worse, Little Bird. No, we will stay here as long as there are enough of the living to buy our goods. And before there are more dead than alive, we will be on to the next town."

Zio pulls his dull knife from the pocket of his leather apron.

"Now give me your foot."

Clouds of red dirt billow into the air as the horses streak across the square. From the steps of the cathedral, I watch the color-clad riders cling for dear life to the beasts' slick backs. The clamor of the crowd is deafening. Waving the bright flags of their *contrade*, the Sienese press forward, those in front nearly trampled by their frenzied neighbors or the thunder of hooves. Within seconds, the horses fly together down an alley as a frantic mass of dirt and rumbling, and the roar of the crowd moves with them.

Zio and Elia have set up their boxes, open to a small display of powders and oils, facing the crowd. In exchange for a few coins, Elia is offering one of her posies—a mixture of rosemary and field flowers—to a lady in a fine robe of indigo.

In the frenzy of the brief horse race, even the ever-present construction alongside the cathedral has come to a halt. The stonemasons, bricklayers, and carpenters have suspended work to watch the horses fly across the cobblestones. In the group of men, I see Paolo sharing a hunk of bread with a brawny, toothless man beside him. From this vantage point, it is easy to see that the cathedral addition will be massive. Paolo has found his own source of livelihood in Siena, as have I, though mine remains a secret.

Then I see her. Lorenzetti's older daughter. She hovers at the top of the stairs, alone. The mean-faced younger sister is nowhere in sight.

"You do this horse race every year?"

She jumps when I speak to her. Her skin looks pale and sallow in spite of the scorch of the midday sun.

"Sometimes twice," she says. "But it is much quieter this year," she says. "Many streets are closed. The *contrada* of Brucco is not even competing. The pestilence has kept many at home."

"And your father...?"

"He and my uncle stayed back in the studio; they have panels to finish. You have seen their work in the cathedral?" she asks. When I shake my head, she gestures for me to follow.

I turn to see if Zio, Elia, or Paolo is watching me, but they have disappeared from view in the pressing mass of race-goers.

Slowly, my eyes adjust to the darkness. I follow Lorenzetti's daughter, letting the cool air of the church interior wash over me. The cathedral is a chamber of echoing footsteps and pigeon wings, lit by dozens of gilded altarpieces shimmering in the candlelight. She stops before a large panel.

"It's the presentation of the Christ child in the temple," she says. I see the child, the holy parents, and the saints around them, but my eyes are on the colors.

"Cinnabar," I say. "Verdigris. Woad."

"Yes," the painter's daughter says. "And also lacquer. Lapis lazuli. And a few other pigments whose origins we don't reveal," she says, raising her chest boastfully again.

"They are all your father's?" I ask, taking in the dozens of the glistening panels around us.

"No, not just our work," she says. "Siena is full of painters. They say it is our sin that has brought the Great Mortality upon us," she says. "And my father and my uncle... They paint to help take away the transgressions of us all." She pauses. "We shall remain occupied for a while, I think."

"I want to stay in Siena," I say suddenly.

The girl turns her dark eyes on me. "Why?"

"It is the most beautiful place I have ever seen," I say. "A place one would be happy to call home."

"Then maybe you will find a way," she says.

"How would I do that?" I feel my shoulders fall.

"You know how to grind pigments," she shrugs. "And we have many painters in Siena. Apothecaries, too. Maybe my father could help you."

As soon as she says the words, I know that I must convince Paolo. That if he understands it as I do, then he will want to stay, too.

"Yes," I say, and my heart is already filled with hope.

But suddenly, Lorenzetti's daughter is not listening. She slumps on a stone bench that lines the side of a chapel. All the color seems to have drained from her face except for a pale shade of green.

"Are you well?" I sit next to her and reach for her arm.

Before she can answer, a wail cuts through the stillness of the church.

Suddenly, a woman lurches into the chapel, barely bolstering a tall man at her side. He threatens to topple her over with the weight of his lanky frame.

"Madonna!" I hear a woman's voice wail again. The sound draws the attention of the stumpy, balding priest, who rushes out of the sacristy toward us.

"Help us, father!" The woman's face is full of panic.

Then, the main door to the cathedral opens, and more ragged souls enter the church. The sick. People are bringing their stricken family members from the crowd outside into the church. I stand as the priest rushes toward the woman and her careening husband.

"Signora! Friends!" The priest's voice is full of desperation. "You cannot bring the afflicted here. Please! You must turn around immediately! Return to your homes!"

The air suddenly fills with moaning, with beseeching prayers, with tears. The painter's daughter hardly notices. Her eyes have turned glassy and she stares forward toward her father's gilded altarpiece, as if entranced.

The squat priest scurries to flush out the crowd, but the woman does not move. Her eyes scan the church, and then settle on me. She pushes the tall man toward me. As he lurches forward, I see seeping, bruise-like pustules on either side of his neck. His eyes stare vacant and black.

"Help us!" She screams at me as the priest attempts to push them backward. But the crowd follows the lady. Suddenly there is a group of ragged, near-dead people crowding around us.

"I beg you," the lady says in a frantic whisper. "Girl with

the stigmata. Lay your hands on my husband. Please! You are our only hope."

Suddenly there is crying and moaning all around me, outstretched hands brushing my shift, reaching for me. Another woman grasps my wrist with a bony hand, trying to press it to the wounds on my palm. My heart beats wildly in my chest and I wrest my hand away from her grip.

I climb onto the stone bench, and, leaving the painter's daughter behind, I rush to the end of the bench and jump over the back of a man kneeling before us.

The hobbling mass of the sick and desperate cannot move as quickly as I can. I rush toward the door and out into the square.

"What has gotten into you, Little Bird?" Even with his long legs, Paolo struggles to keep up.

"Come."

For the first time in my life, I believe that we might live without Zio. I have done my best already to explain it to Paolo. Now I must show him.

"Wait." Paolo reaches for my shoulder, and spins me around to face him. "What you are suggesting is not possible. We cannot stay here. I owe a debt to Zio, as do you."

I blink. "Paolo. He has been keeping your money. My money. Do you see? The opportunity to change our lives for the better is now. Let them go if they want. But you and I... we might stay in Siena. You can work here. Signor Lorenzetti might help us. His daughter has said so herself. He is a kind man."

He struggles for words. "Little Bird. You don't know what I have done."

Slowly, he reaches for his cap. For the first time ever, I watch him remove it. I see the slickness of the dark hair across the crown of his head, and his lined forehead. Across his brow, an angry red scar in the shape of an M cuts into the skin in deep grooves.

Malefactor.

I am silent for a few minutes, letting the truth set in. He has been marked with a branding iron.

A thief? A murderer? Is that why he fled Naples on the first wagon that came through town?

My mind quickly reviews the years I have known Paolo, years in which I have witnessed only hard work and loyalty.

"Do you see, Little Bird?" he says. "Who will have me?"

I look into his eyes. "*Anyone* would be lucky to have you, Paolo. Keep your hat on." I push his cap back over his forehead and yank on his hand so hard that he stumbles.

But when we move into the artist's *contrada*, things have changed. There are no more flags flapping from the windows. No more tables in the streets. No more crowds. The windows are shuttered, the doors battened. Paolo hesitates. A skinny cat darts past our legs.

As we turn into the artist's street, I hesitate, too. At that moment, a cloud obscures the sun.

At the artist's studio, a large wooden cross has been nailed over the door.

Before the great colored marble façade of the cathedral, I slump onto the stairs. Paolo heaves himself beside me, placing his hands heavy on my shoulders. In that instant, I join the aggrieved citizens of Siena, those who have lost someone important to them. Finally, I am part of a community. I feel as though I might fall to the ground.

I press my ragged palms over my eyes, not able to bear the thought of the painter and his family closed behind those doors. Sick. Or worse.

"I'm sorry, Little Bird." Paolo's voice is soft and gentle in my ear. He takes my hands in his. I feel his rough carpenter's palms against my ragged scars and scabs. "The pestilence is spreading. I think you are a brave girl, but we cannot stay here. Do you see now?"

Suddenly, a great shriek rings out across the cathedral square.

"It is them!"

I raise my head to see the hefty pork seller moving across the *campo*. Behind her, a group of market sellers follows. "That cure seller and his friends!" I turn to look for the object of her tirade, but the cathedral steps are empty, except for us.

The woman strides toward us, a fist in the air. "You! You have brought the Great Mortality to us! It was you the whole time!"

Paolo and I stand.

"Where is that charlatan cure seller and his old white hag?" Her face is a twisted, red picture of rage. "You have brought this horror upon us, you and your false cures! And *you*!" she screams, her twisted face and a fat finger set at me. "You are a lie! You have deceived all of us! You are marked by the Devil! Leave now or we will see that you are thrown into the pits with the rest of them!"

The crowd presses forward, full of fury. Neither of us can find a word to say. Paolo reaches for my hand this time, and we start running.

Behind, there are angry voices. Ahead, only death.

At the city gates, the corpse carts stand in disarray, one overturned. Two hay barrows are loaded with bodies stiff and pale—women, men, children, a cleric in a brown habit.

A frenzied swarm of flies buzzes so loudly that my ears hurt, and the stench causes us both to retch uncontrollably as we pass. One of the corpse-bearers himself is slumped in the dirt, purple, oozing boils protruding from under his ears. There is no one left to carry the bodies to the pits.

Blinking back tears, I watch my feet run through a blur of death. We run as fast as our legs will carry us, through the open gates, and down the red earthen path into the fields. We run until we are well beyond the walls, out in the plain where our wagon stands under the oak tree. Zio and Elia have already hitched the mule.

I pull on Paolo's sleeve, and we stop, gasping for air.

"Wait."

"*Tutto bene*?" he asks, panting.

I nod.

Paolo watches me carefully for a moment, then turns and heads toward the wagon. I feel the weight of watching him walk away. Still, I hesitate.

Zio checks the hitches on the harness, and watches me hawk-like from behind the mule's muzzle. He says nothing. His face looks drawn and gaunt.

I turn back to look at the tall spire looming over the city walls of Siena, a city so shining and beautiful. So full of hope for us, for the future, for opportunity. So overcome by death.

"*Andiamo*, Little Bird." I hear Elia's familiar voice call from the wagon. She opens a flap in the oilcloth and her pale hand summons me.

Paolo turns to look at me, squinting in the sunlight. *Are you coming*? He doesn't say it out loud, but I hear it all the same.

Finally, I take a deep breath and walk toward them. Elia helps me climb into the back of the wagon. I sink my back into a bag full of linen. I feel the wheels begin to creak and turn under my body.

For hours, no one speaks. I watch the parched landscape unfurl before us, a vast tapestry of deserted towns, open pits, and bonfires of clothing, bedding, and furniture. Stinking, warm breezes waft over abandoned fields.

As the sun rises high and hot in the afternoon haze, Zio falls forward at the reins. Paolo manages to catch him before he drops to the ground from the driver's bench.

We stop.

Elia nurses Zio for the rest of the day, emptying our vials of oils and pressing dried herbs into the virulent black sores that have appeared suddenly under his arms. She whispers to him and rocks him on her lap while Paolo paces in the tall grass.

By nightfall, our box of cures is empty.

Paolo digs a shallow grave beside the road. Elia tosses our last bouquets of dried lavender and oregano in after the body, and we mumble a quiet benediction before moving on.

At dawn, our wooden wheels shudder into the ruts far beyond the walls of Siena.

Paolo makes a clicking noise with his tongue, and our mule trudges forward. The now-familiar hills of Tuscany begin to flatten out into long stretches of fallow fields. Elia sits between the bundles, her face buried in her hands, as the hills recede from view. I move into the driver's bench alongside Paolo.

"Where shall we go, Little Bird?" Paolo asks, after a long period of silence. The old mule flicks her ears backward, listening to the new voices above the rattle of the wheels.

No one has ever asked me this question before. The farther away we move from Siena, the clearer my mind becomes. I rub my palms together, where the scabs have crusted over and the red pigment has begun to fade.

"North," I say. "Venice. We will sell our powders there. Pigments. Many different colors that painters will use to make beautiful things. Perhaps we will stay."

Paolo snaps the rein and the mule picks up her pace, sending up a cloud of dirt. I imagine that I see Paolo grimace, but I am never sure. His wounds remain on the inside.

We crest the ridge, and across the landscape before us, trails of smoke from small pyres curl into the sky.

Inspiration of Laura Morelli's Little Bird

After Saint Francis of Assisi was marked with the stigmata in 1224, many others across central Italy claimed to have received these special signs of Christ's crucifixion—whether divinely given, imagined, or faked. The Great Mortality, as it was called when it ravaged Tuscany in the summer of 1348, wiped out more than half the population of the region's prosperous cities, including Pisa, where the scourge may have entered via merchant ships in port.

Siena's residents struggled long after the horror of the Black Death came to an end. The city never fully regained its political and economic dominance. Its ambitious cathedral construction project was halted and never finished. Ambrogio Lorenzetti, who was working with his brother Pietro on several important painting commissions in the city at the time, hastily scrawled his last testament to his wife and daughters on a piece of parchment on June 9, 1348, and then disappeared from the historical record.

Apart from these established facts, the band of misfits who hawk their cures in Siena's medieval *campi* are figments of my own imagination.

Learn more about Laura Morelli at https://lauramorelli.com

Footsteps

By J. K. Knauss

Sevilla
1350

The Moors in Sevilla may have been our mortal enemies, but I can't fault anything they built in this city. The narrow streets provide relief from the unrelenting sun. Their splendid church, which we Christians use now, has a tower with wide ramps anyone can ascend to view all the wonders of Sevilla at once, as if we were the great storks that fly in to roost at dusk. My Alfonso's great-grandfather, for whom he was named, is entombed there, and sometimes I'm permitted to take the short walk accompanied by a guard to light candles and say prayers for him. The gardens here in the royal palace carry my worries away on bubbling fountains and fragrances of orange, honeysuckle, and jasmine. My room in the Christian part of the palace has elegant vaulted ceilings and colorful painted tile walls, but whenever I'm allowed, I like to come to the old quarters, where Almohad hands crafted delicate arcs and curlicues into plaster and channeled calming currents like brooks across the floor.

It's a beautiful prison.

Some mornings, a cooing dove or a strutting peacock brings me to a state that is not quite waking, and I believe I can feel Alfonso's weight on the bed, hear him sigh in the uneasy slumber of a king. For an instant, Spain is ours, he's still at my side, and the nightmare is over. Those are the worst mornings. When I understand that the sensation was only the dearest hope of my heart, I have to relive those last days and try to fathom why God took him away from me, away from Spain, so suddenly, so brutally.

We were in Gibraltar only four months ago, besieging the city for the fifth time, as I thought was right. But God must not have agreed. After Alfonso and I set up camp and sent our demands, nothing changed. We blocked their fresh water and sank their supply ships, but Gibraltar must've been populated with ghouls who needed no mortal sustenance. The Great Dying took half of our foot soldiers, and it seemed we would never win the city back from Granada's pagan hands, but even so, Alfonso had faced worse. I didn't know why he was acting more irritable than I'd ever seen him.

"We should ask the King of Portugal to send reinforcements," said the commander in the strategy tent that evening, the Monday before Easter.

Alfonso slammed his hand on the table and swept a wineskin off it. "I don't know why I've brought any of you here. You're all against me!" he shouted. He stomped on the wineskin, soaking the straw flooring and splattering the boots of his trusted advisors and generals. The men remained silent. None of them were accustomed to such an outburst. Alfonso hadn't acted like that since before I met him, twenty years ago.

In his rage, he reached for the map of the city spread out on the table. I knew if he mangled it, the cause was lost, so I stayed his hand with the lightest caress. "There, there, my love," I murmured. "That's enough for today. Let's get some rest. I'll write to your sons tomorrow and they'll come and help us. We'll win Gibraltar in time for Easter feasting."

His blue eyes regarded me from between stray strands of golden hair. I saw no recognition, so I sent the men away and grasped his hand. It burned me, but the light returned to his eyes.

"Leonor, Leonor," he said. "I ache all over, inside and out."

Another winter ailment, I was sure. After all, he was thirty-eight years old and had been a warrior for nearly all of them. A body can only take so much before it demands rest. I walked Alfonso to our private tent the way one leads a skittish horse. I undressed him and arranged the blankets to make a cradle for him, but not cover him. He was too hot. The bed strings groaned as he contorted in search of relief.

I took up the enormous peacock fan by the bed, but I was too exhausted to imagine fanning my love all night long. I thought I'd been through everything he had and had earned my rest, too. I went to the door and whispered to the page standing guard. "Come and keep the king cool while he rests." The page was wearing mittens and a heavy cloak to guard against the night and must've wondered why the king was too warm, but he obeyed silently.

I left my dress on for modesty and to avoid catching a chill from the fan. I lay next to Alfonso and smoothed the hair over his brow.

"I love you," I barely heard him say. Maybe he never said it and I'm only wishing he had. He kissed me with the passion of first love—or last love? Did he know what was happening?

I fell asleep quickly, untroubled, in spite of the incessant fanning, in spite of my darling's constant movement and groans of misery. I didn't hear them then, but now those groans accompany me everywhere, a prison I can never escape from.

I woke in the dark to the sound of my name.

"Lady Leonor, awake! Lady Leonor, what do I do?" the page whimpered.

"Leonor! Leonor!" Alfonso bellowed as he thrashed the blankets to the floor.

"I'm here, my love," I said.

"Help," he said in greatest secrecy. "Tell those devils to stop pulling on me. Tell the angels to kill the devils forever. Then I can sleep. Thank you, darling."

I reached out and my hand came to rest on my love's

neck. It was not the prickly bearded skin I knew so well. It hardly felt like skin at all, only sickness, something untouchable from the forest floor.

"Bring a torch from outside," I told the page, and when he did, I regretted it. The firelight confirmed what my hand had felt, what I never imagined could happen to my love, the king. He'd survived battles, freak storms, hunger, thirst, and two years of losing our people to the plague God sent to punish—I thought—only the poor laborers and the lowest of the low. Why would God want to strike him with that filth when Alfonso had never done anything but God's will?

"My love, did you visit the foot soldiers?" I asked.

"Send them away! They're dragging me to Hell with them. I won't go!"

"He did visit them, my lady, three days ago," the page said.

"Why?"

"He wanted to raise spirits after the Great Dying."

Where had I been? Why hadn't I stopped him?

"Leonor, Leonor!" Alfonso writhed in my arms.

"Should I go for the physician?" asked the page.

I sat up. "He can do nothing. What happens now is God's will," I told the page and myself. "Don't bother to tell the commanders or anyone else, either. In the morning, we'll all know exactly what God wants." I had the page take the torch back outside so I wouldn't have to watch my love's suffering.

I held Alfonso fast for the rest of that eternal night. I kept him still as he fought the demons only he saw. I whispered in his ear, smoothed his hair, and kissed his sweet face. After hours that seemed like days, he stopped struggling. "Alfonso, darling," I whispered.

I held my fingers to his lips to feel what he said. "Leonor."

The breath of life was still in him, though it became shallow. I had the impression that his spirit, the human being God had made in the likeness of His perfection, had fled the putrid body so it became a hollow, useless shell even as it shuddered and sighed. And I loved it still, because it had been his body.

Tears cascaded from my eyes to warm his face. I don't know when Alfonso XI, king of my heart, took his last breath, only that it was in the dark, and that he did not pass on alone. The best part of my own soul went with him.

I still held the body close to me, weeping silently, when the first rays of light of that Tuesday before Easter filtered through the tent's canvas. I had last kissed my love's face what seemed like decades before and had become as still as he.

The page opened the tent flap to four or five of the commanders, who stopped speaking among themselves mid-sentence. When I think about what they must've seen, I'm blasphemous: I must've looked like Mary cradling her beloved Son when He descended from the Cross. Her love for our Savior was not greater than mine for Alfonso.

One of the commanders strode to the bed and pulled the king out of my arms—something I would've thought impossible. "The king is dead! The plague has taken him!"

Amid confused gasps and exclamations, another of the commanders spoke sense: "We must tell the queen."

It felt as though the entire tent fell away and every soldier left alive in the camp were staring at Alfonso's corpse, and then at me, their gazes burning holes in the fabric of my dress.

I was presented at Alfonso's court in Sevilla when I was a young widow, but he had married María of Portugal two years before. I often wondered why the instant, permanent bond arose between us at such an awkward time. But the queen never offered an opinion and never helped when she easily could have, when the Catalans left the Canary Islands and Portugal wanted them. So it was only natural that Alfonso turned to me time after time. He rewarded me for the children I gave him and my counsel with lands and titles until I became a permanent fixture at court and more of a companion to him than Queen María would ever be.

My tears ran out with the shock. Without the king to stand next to, what was my place? Where were my children? Only they could help me in a world without their father.

Someone led me to my ladies' tent, where I looked down to find the front of my dress covered with blood and pus. One of my ladies took it off me and replaced it with a fresh one, and I wish she hadn't. I haven't been able to find that dress since. She probably burned it, and the dress I wore when I last held my true love went up in smoke.

The commanders broke the siege and made ready to return north without consulting me. For all the asking I did, I couldn't confirm where they intended to bury Alfonso, but when I climbed into the wagon next to his wasted shell, no one said anything.

I'm not sure how many days I bumped and jostled in that wagon, possibly four or five. I don't know how or if Easter was observed among the troops. At Jerez de la Frontera, embalmers removed Alfonso's entrails. I placed their box in a niche in the royal chapel in the palace there, and masses were sung. They sounded all wrong, the tones coming in too high or too low, hollow.

The commanders acted quickly, keen to bring the body to the queen and their son, Pedro, in Sevilla to secure the royal succession, but I was in no condition to notice details. Only my most faithful servants bothered to keep me alive with food that might've been the finest on offer, but it tasted like nothing on my tongue and felt coarse in my throat. It was almost too much effort to swallow, to breathe. The only thing that came effortlessly was thought. Holding my surviving children in my mind made me strong. There were eight of them, all with noble titles, and the queen had only one son. I could never be the queen, but I could become the queen mother.

By the time we approached the royal palace in Sevilla, I had thought about the encounter so many times, I almost believed it had already taken place. I would send the queen back to Portugal, where she belonged, and her Pedro could go with her and keep her company. Even the queen's guards should obey my orders because I had been at the king's side in life and in death. Who knew what he wanted better than I?

Our cortege pulled up before the queen and Pedro and their court in the entrance patio as if they had been waiting for us all along. But no, they were only waiting for Alfonso's cold remains. Queen María refused to look at me, turning her veiled face to the linen-wrapped cadaver at my side. Her thin hands prodded at the shoulders as if she could wake him. It was something I'd tried many times before I had to pray over the entrails in Jerez. Since she hadn't seen his buboes, heard his delirious shouting, or felt his blood on her dress, I couldn't blame her.

"María," I said, still seated in the cart, still in possession of Alfonso, towering over her.

From the bewilderment of grief, her face flashed to unabashed rage. The movement was obvious even under the veil. Before she could give voice to her thoughts, her mountainous squire Fernández de Olmedo clasped her and guided her away, and her son, the new King Pedro himself, extended his hand to me to help me down from the cart.

"Leonor," he said, looking for all the world like a fifteen-year-old, taller version of my Alfonso, with that flop of blond hair and sympathy in his gaze.

I took his hand and stepped down, and before my shoes hit the cobblestones, he had his arms around me. I pushed back at first, but Pedro's embrace was gentle, and I dissolved into his musculature like salt in water.

"I couldn't save him," I blubbered. "I did what I could, but the plague can't be stopped. Only the Great Dying could've taken your father. No one could've slain him in battle. He would've lived forever!"

"I know," Pedro said. He pulled away, and I interred my tears in my hands. "Leonor, we'll bury my father here in Sevilla, and we'll give you rooms here in the palace. You're the mother of the only siblings I have, but please, try not to cross my mother. She told me to send you into exile."

80

Pedro is right, I need to avoid the queen. But the sympathy I have for him is the kind of affection any child would elicit in a mother like me. Even and especially with the regents he has to influence him, he'll never be the decisive warrior ruler his father was.

When I first arrived here, I wrote letters to each of my children to tell them how their father had died—valiantly, confessed, and at peace with God—and how I was living in the palace in Sevilla—comfortably but missing them. Then, awaiting their responses, I took to strolling about the palace and happening to end up in the Chamber of Justice. It's the latest addition. My Alfonso had Moorish craftsmen build it with an extraordinary coffered ceiling and intricate plaster walls with Castilian coats of arms.

It's also where I listen in on what María and Pedro's regents tell him. One morning, I happened to arrive in the doorway especially early, and Pedro was still alone. He'd taken to his royal responsibilities with admirable earnestness, and he stood in the center of the chamber wringing his hands. When he looked up from the fountain he'd been studying so intently, relief washed over his round face.

"Lady Leonor, I'm so confused. What would Father have done?"

Stunned, it took me a moment to realize this was my moment to stride toward him and take his hand. "What's the matter?" I asked the boy, then added, "my king," as an afterthought.

"Half my advisors think we should support the House of Valois against England, and the rest think we should side with the Plantagenets. Honestly, I don't know why they don't make peace," he explained with a slight lisp. "They each have enough problems in their own countries with the lack of laborers. They lose more every day to the Great Dying, just like we do."

I let go of his hand so he wouldn't feel my urgency. It was vital he take my advice, but he would surely flee me if I frightened him with the forcefulness Alfonso had always admired.

"Your father, who had this magnificent chamber built to discuss just this kind of issue, valued loyalty highly. England has always been our ally, especially since Eleanor's marriage to King Edward was so successful. But perhaps equally important, the English buy most of the wool produced in Castile, even after the arrival of the plague. Many fields lie fallow and at the last Cortes, half of the monasteries and towns were unable to pay their tributes or send the soldiers we needed because there just wasn't the same number of people as there was before. If we were to suddenly make enemies of the English, the economy of the Central Meseta would irreparably collapse."

"Oh." He looked startled in spite of my best efforts.

I gave him a reassuring smile. "Not to worry. You're the king. You can prevent all of that simply by staying loyal to the English cause. Whatever they ask for, they've earned it with their friendship over these many years. That's what your father would say," I finished, rather than "That's what I would tell your father."

A great commotion of footsteps interrupted our confidence, and Queen María and Fernández de Olmedo passed into the grand archway with other noble regents behind. Although her leathery squire dwarfed her, María drew herself to her full height when she saw me and seemed to fill the chamber. I thought lightning bolts would rain down from the coffered ceiling as she shouted at me, but she surprised me by gently touching Fernández de Olmedo's hand and saying so low I barely heard, "Please escort Lady Leonor back to her chamber."

When Fernández de Olmedo's hulk advanced toward me, my heart nearly leapt out of my chest. "I'll go!" I shrilled. "I'll leave the king to his business. Thank you for your time, Your Majesty."

I caught Pedro's eye as I turned to the archway, but before I could be sure he'd take my advice, Fernández de Olmedo lumbered between us. I strode back to my room, keeping well ahead of the queen's squire as he trailed me. I took it into my head that his touch was poisonous to me, that if he reached me, I would break out in boils and buboes and perish as painfully as my love.

Perhaps Alfonso could've spent more time with Pedro and taught him to rule properly even if he didn't take to it naturally. But since the queen keeps me from him so I can't set his father's example for him, the only remedy now will have to come from my children. They did benefit from Alfonso's love and guidance.

After that day, I've tried to stay in the doorway behind the council's back, and if Queen María sees me, I casually gather up my skirts and head to the gardens, feeling her gaze bore into my back the whole way. The bits and pieces of news I gather from those moments are my small triumphs over a woman I didn't realize would defend her position so jealously.

One morning, far too long after my arrival, the maid they've given me had just finished braiding my hair and arranging my headpiece when Pedro appeared, looking even more serious than when he took advice in the Chamber of Justice.

"What is it," I asked, "my king?"

"Enrique Alfonso of Castile, Lord of the County of Noreña, Count of Trastámara, Lord of Lemos, Sarria, Cabrera, and Ribera, to see you, Lady Leonor."

My Enrique, my eldest surviving son, the third I gave Alfonso, emerged from behind the archway with the confident grin that would give him away anywhere. I held him, making sure he was still as hale as I'd last seen him. I wiped the tears from my eyes—much sweeter than the tears I cried most days—and observed the half-brothers standing together. Enrique was only a couple of years older than Pedro, and yet he was already a man, full of his father's vigor and strength, but with my darker coloring. Enrique was the eldest of a pair, but thank God, he lacked the telltale thinness and weakness that marked most twins I'd known.

"I'll let you two share your stories," lisped Pedro.

"Thank you, my king, for bringing my son to me," I said as he left.

I crushed Enrique to me again. This time I never intended to let go. "And your brothers and sister? How are they? Haven't they received my letters?"

"They've all written back to you, as far as I know. Fadrique wanted to come with me, but I told him only one of us at a time should be absent from our holdings."

"You're right, of course. Has the queen seen you? Pedro seemed to treat you well."

"The queen mother didn't deign to see me." He slipped away to pace the chamber. "Mother, are you a prisoner? Is this a room in a palace or a dungeon?"

"Look at it this way: at least I'm alive. God knows I haven't always wanted to be alive since the Great Dying took your father, but María or even Pedro could've accused me of any number of things. Most importantly, you and your brothers and sister are alive, too, and still hold your titles. All of it could have been taken away as soon as your father was no longer there to defend you."

"I see neither your grief nor your imprisonment have dulled your political acumen. But while my father lived, why did you never ask him to divorce María or put her away? Then I would be the king now, and Pedro would be the one shrouded in uncertainty. You saw us together. Who looks like the legitimate one?"

He spoke the truth, but too loudly in my prison. "Don Juan Manuel once advised me to demand an annulment," I said, equally loudly, hoping someone else would hear. "But I knew putting María away would've started a war with Portugal, and we've always needed our cousins to the west as our allies against the pagans in Granada. I suspect Juan Manuel didn't have Castile's best interests at heart. I went into seclusion at the convent of San Clemente when you were young, after your brother Juan was born, just to prove to Portugal that María was a valued royal partner to your father."

"Shortly after we won the Battle of Salado River with Portuguese help, my sister Juana was born. You weren't much of a nun, Mother."

I crossed the room to whisper in Enrique's ear, that flesh that was mine and Alfonso's, a living testament to our love. "We can't speak freely here, my son and future king. I think someone is always listening to me."

"So it is that bad for you," he whispered back. "Do they suspect you're not going to conform to their wishes? Should I try to get you out of here?"

"No. Here is where I can stay on top of what happens at court, even if they don't want me to. You can best help me by doing something else. I want you to get married."

He startled but kept his voice under control. "Married? To whom?"

"Don Juan Manuel is dead now, so his political machinations can't hurt us anymore. His daughter is the heiress to the lordship of Vizcaya and the great-granddaughter of King Fernando the Saint. A marriage between you would make you rich and wildly strengthen your legitimacy for the throne, and she's about your age. It would really be best for Spain. Please consider it."

"Of course I will, Mother, if you think it's best," he murmured. "When have you ever been wrong?"

"I couldn't save your father," I moaned. "We never should've gone to Gibraltar!"

Enrique held me for moments that were far too short while I wailed, shamelessly pitying myself. I heard swift footsteps, and Fernández de Olmedo and another of the queen's squires—just who I'd wanted to witness the scene—arrived at the chamber door.

"King Pedro wants to see Don Enrique," said Fernández de Olmedo.

"Right now," said the other.

"I'll do everything I can to ensure your comfort,"

Enrique said, holding my face in his hands. "Stay strong."

When he drew away, I cried, "I love you, my darling son!" and prostrated myself on the bed until I was sure the queen's men were gone.

It's August and the only remedy against the heat is to press my cheek to the cold tile floor. I'm not allowed into the chambers with fountains anymore, and no maid comes to dress me or braid my hair.

Although I will never recover what I lost when Alfonso died in my arms, after Enrique's visit, I had new hope for my future as a powerful influence on the Castilian crown. I continued to sulk about the palace, making sure everyone close to the queen saw how distraught I was, and in this way, I overheard news about the war with Granada and about my children. Then one day, news that was no surprise to me arrived in a surprising way.

The curtain was drawn across the archway into my chamber. I was lying in bed, still unable to sleep through to the morning after four months, wondering when my maid would appear to start the day. I heard footsteps, but they were too hurried to be my maid. The curtain snapped open and the queen charged to the side of my bed so quickly I hardly had time to sit up. Fernández de Olmedo trudged after her and I gathered blankets about me to shield against him.

"How dare you?" Queen María seethed. "After everything we've done for you. Did you think we wouldn't notice you were plotting to overthrow Pedro?" Her normally white face was as green as my sheets, as if she had been possessed by a dragon demon.

"Overthrow?" I choked.

"Your son Enrique married Juana Manuel de Villena, heiress of Vizcaya, four days ago. Go ahead. Explain to me how that doesn't make his lands, resources, and soldiers equal to or greater than Pedro's."

I was thrilled Enrique had followed my advice, and so quickly. I couldn't think fast enough for the queen.

"Your hand is all over this," she hissed, using unexpected strength to force the blankets off me.

I pulled my shift over my knees, but Fernández de Olmedo's gaze still devoured my body.

"You're wrong," I said. "This is news to me, too. How could I have arranged a marriage from here? I'm in no condition to think of such things, anyway." I thought of the warmth of Alfonso's lips the last time he spoke my name to start a flow of fat, hot tears.

"Enrique never met Juana Manuel before. Why would it occur to him to marry her? And he's only seventeen. Why the hurry to marry anyone?"

The queen's insight bewildered me. I'd had no idea who I was up against. At this crucial moment, almost naked before her and her poisonous accessory, I was speechless.

Queen María glanced at Fernández de Olmedo and his hairy arms reached toward me. I shrank from him. "No. I'll go wherever you want me to," I told the queen. "But don't let him touch me."

Almost suffocating under their folds, I carried my own dresses to this windowless room where one of the queen's men guards me day and night. I haven't received any visitors since I moved here. I think even Pedro has been told to stay away. Do they think I would try to kill him here in my prison cell? I'm permitted to move about the palace, but only if accompanied by the guard on duty. More often than not, it seems to be Fernández de Olmedo, so I spend most of my time here, hoping my children know how much of a threat Queen María has turned out to be. I pray to Christ, His mother, the apostles, and Saint Clement to send word to my children that now, yes, now I need their help.

Talavera de la Reina
1351

Talavera de la Reina—The Queen's City on the River. Alfonso granted this place to Queen María when they married. I hate it.

I'm surrounded by some of the strongest walls in all Castile, trapped in a square tower in a castle built by Moors when this place was theirs. The daylight hardly hits my face through the arrow slots, and I shiver under rough wool blankets. My only human contact is Fernández de Olmedo's stone face as he looks in on me or brings food I can hardly choke down because I wonder if it's poisoned. The terror he used to provoke in me has subsided. He never says much of anything. I might as well talk to these walls.

Queen María lives here in the castle with us. Although she never visits me, I feel her presence like a weight on my chest. If she leaves the castle for even a few hours, I take advantage to breathe more freely, but even then, it's as if the walls obey her command to keep vigil on me. I think I see them come closer in every day, gradually squeezing the air out of the room until one day, I suffocate.

In January, Queen María came to my room in the palace in Sevilla. I heard Fernández de Olmedo's heavy footsteps outside the door come to a stop to listen in. The queen told me she and Pedro were traveling to the Cortes to be held in Valladolid.

"We'll pass through lands held by the Order of Santiago," she said, strolling about the chamber without looking at me. "Pedro thought you might like to join us."

"Will I be able to see Fadrique?"

"Ah, that's right. Enrique's twin is the Grand Master of the Order of Santiago. Perhaps something can be arranged. We'll certainly let him know where you'll be." She looked over her shoulder at what must've been my hopeful expression and smirked. And still I didn't suspect what was to come. Thoughts of seeing Fadrique after so many meaningless months of hardly feeling like I'd ever had children at all obliterated my reasoning.

It started innocuously. They gave me back the maid to help me pack and make me more elegant for the journey. They gave me my own covered wagon so I could bundle up against the winter. But we made it no further than Alcalá del Río, only a half-day's journey even in the wet weather we'd started in, when the convoy came to a halt in the middle of the town square. Fernández de Olmedo parted my curtains and reached toward me. I leaped out the other side only to be confronted with what might've been several days of plague victims, blighted corpses laid out in two neat rows, awaiting transport to a crematorium or mass grave. I covered my mouth in dismay. I'd had no idea the Great Dying was so close to Sevilla.

Two others of the queen's guards found me and took me by the arms to stand on the other side of my wagon, where what was left of the town had gathered around the fountain and were kneeling before Pedro. It was the first time I'd seen the king in months, and he had grown into his role considerably, accepting his subjects' demonstrations of loyalty with a regal wave of the hand and squinted eyes.

Beside Pedro, his mother watched me arrive. She strode to me with her arm outstretched and I understood I had to take her hand. She looked me in the eyes while she announced to the townspeople, "Look! It's Leonor Núñez de Guzmán, a noble native of Sevilla. You may remember, she used to spend a lot of time with King Alfonso, may he rest in peace. Come, Leonor."

The queen's grip nearly pulverized my hand before she led me to Pedro. I tried to read the king's face, but too quickly, Queen María used the surprising power in her hand to clutch my shoulder painfully, pressing against bone, and push down so that I had little choice but to kneel before Pedro. The applause started out tepid, but the queen raised her arms. "Observe how ambition bows before legitimacy!" The townspeople clapped harder and added some shouts and whistles I tried hard not to listen to until Queen María was satisfied.

They never threw rocks or anything else, but my skin felt

as bruised as if they had. I climbed back into my wagon, dreading the next town. And I was right. We stopped everywhere with enough survivors to gather a crowd, sometimes two or three a day, and it was always the same, except that I came out of the wagon before Fernández de Olmedo had a chance to open the curtain.

And except for Llerena. The retinue was welcomed into the palace of the Grand Master of the Order of Santiago in Llerena almost as if the past year had never taken place. I saw Fadrique framed by archways, the image of his twin, Enrique, a commanding presence with his hands on his hips, and it took my breath away to think this warrior was my son. The astonishment didn't last long, because when he caught sight of me, he ran across the courtyard, passing Pedro and the queen as if they weren't there, to catch me up in his arms.

I gave myself over to the sensations of the moment, inhaling the scent of his hair and velvet tunic, letting him kiss my cheeks and hands. I knew that even if Spain had already forgotten what we had done to keep its people safe from the Aragonese, the Moors, and their own ruthless nobles, Alfonso and I were immortalized in our children.

While observing royal protocols and ensuring Pedro and Queen María wanted for nothing, Fadrique managed to make me feel I could look to my side and see his father sitting there. Everything made sense as my son served a feast as great as before the plague arrived. I didn't even stop to wonder how he managed to make it seem as if there had been no unusual casualties.

That evening, Fadrique showed me to a chamber that had to be bigger and better furnished than the ones he'd given Pedro and Queen María and sat with me by the fireplace, murmuring over the life-sustaining cracks and pops. He told me news about his brothers and sister, eying the door. Finally, he leaned in close.

"We've all heard the way they're parading you through Castile on the way to the Cortes in Valladolid. We can't allow this."

I took his hands in mine. "I do need your help, darling. I've thought of little else. But I can't allow any of you to risk your lands, titles, or lives. That's what it would mean to help me. The best thing for you all to do is support Enrique every way you can. Your father and I taught him well, and I'm confident he'll do what's best for Spain."

"We do, of course we all do, Mother," said Fadrique, and I will never forget the look of love and devotion he gave me. "By the way, Enrique is very happy with Juana Manuel. Do you think you could arrange a marriage like that for me?"

I chuckled ruefully into my collar. "I'll see what I can do." I kissed his forehead.

I didn't sleep well, in spite of the comfort and hope Fadrique had provided. The sound of Fernández de Olmedo's footsteps pacing outside my chamber door all night was a constant reminder of my powerlessness.

I lived on that short meeting for the next fifteen days as the Spain Alfonso and I had shared became a ceaseless succession of merciless strangers who applauded my humiliation before someone my true love had raised me above.

I assumed we would stay in Valladolid until the Cortes came to an end and hoped I would find a way to talk to some of the sympathetic nobles. But the queen must've read my mind. She didn't even stay with her son while he governed, but ushered me here to her city, her fortress, which they say was built by the invincible hand of Abderrahman.

The towers cast a shadow over my cart as we entered Talavera and I knew that evening in Llerena was the last time I would see any of my children. Since that day I haven't seen the outside of this chamber. I escape only in the dreams I've taken to having all times of day. Asleep, I see and touch my Alfonso as he was before Gibraltar and glimpse the futures of my children. With my eyes closed, I witness the growth of my grandchildren and Spain's recovery from the Great Dying.

I loved a king. I helped him bring our nation safely

through tragedies no king has ever seen before. I bore him ten children. I watched him die in a gruesome act of God. I've wished more times than I can count that I had died there with him.

I've made it this far only to face death alone, but I've seen it in dreams: my children will start a new royal line and lead Spain to glory.

For now, I listen to Fernández de Olmedo's muffled footsteps as he paces the hall and wonder when he's coming in to kill me.

Inspiration of J. K. Knauss's Footsteps

A resident of Zamora, Spain, J. K. Knauss has been writing fiction set in medieval Spain with the support of the multiple accolade–winning Low Writers of Tucson, Arizona, ever since she completed her PhD in medieval Spanish literature. Her epic novel, *Seven Noble Knights*, is based on legendary events that may have taken place in the formative tenth century. When she thinks of the effects of the Black Death in Spain, Leonor's fascinating character and long-lasting legacy always come to mind.

Leonor Núñez de Guzmán y Ponce de León was the most powerful and influential woman in Castile while King Alfonso XI was alive. She gave birth to ten of his children while his wife, María of Portugal, had only two. After his death, María held Leonor captive in Sevilla, which must've been a satisfying way to exercise her power as the legitimate widow. Although the new King Pedro was sympathetic to Leonor and tried to find a place for her at court, her ambitions got the best of her. Her plots to take back her previous power included colluding with her son Enrique against María and Pedro. When María found out about the plots, life got successively worse for Leonor until the queen's squire, Fernández de Olmedo, killed her. Leonor was never accused of or tried for any crimes. Her death, viewed as an assassination, was the last reason Enrique needed to justify his claim to the throne, and civil war broke out. After many years of struggle, Enrique became the first king of the Trastámara line, which would eventually give the world Isabel la Católica.

Learn   more   about   J.K.   Knauss   at https://www.jessicaknauss.com

On All Our Houses

By David Blixt

Gargagnago, Italy
20 September, 1362

In my youth, I imagined what Death was like. I tried to picture my own death. I remember hoping for a "good" death. As if there could be such a thing.

When I was knighted, almost fifty years ago, I thought about Death the way the young do. An abstract thing, poetic and even beautiful. Because it was impossible. Even after barely surviving two desperate battles, I didn't ascribe my continued existence to luck. No, I felt immortal. I simply could not imagine the world without me in it, so Death was a fascinating concept. Like Magic, or Angels.

Or Hell.

I suppose Father's work had something to do with my thoughts on Death. How could it not? After all, Dante Alighieri was the world's foremost authority on it. He had actually journeyed to Hell and back—or so everyone believed. I still recall them spitting when he walked by, making the sign to ward off the Evil Eye behind their backs. After first asking for his autograph, of course, or a clipping from his beard. People are contradictory.

Today I think of Death differently. I'm not so old as to see the hooded figure with the scythe as a friend. He's not a comfort. No, I see him as I see the Night, or the Winter. Inevitable. Inexorable. No matter how you bank your fire, you eventually run out of fuel and freeze.

It is a terrible thing to feel that chill before your own time. When it is the chill of others. I don't fear my own death. It's the death of those I love that terrifies me.

Death's chill is in the house now. And I'm not the warrior to fight him. I'm helpless. No sword can drive him off. No law can reason him into submission. No passionate fire can beat him back. There is nothing to be done.

There is nothing worse than nothing.

On the floor at my feet is the crest of my family, white against gold marble. I was so proud when I had it lain in. I'd designed the new crest myself.

Now it seems to mock me. A single angel's wing, fanned right to left, as if preparing for flight. Flights of angels. The root of my family name is *aliger*, meaning "moving with the speed of flight." Like the little wings of Mercury.

The little Mercury...

A hand rests on my shoulder. "Pietro."

I glance up, startled. It's Petrarch, dressed and ready for our walk. He's come from Padua to share my suffering. I did the same for him last year. I understand now the burden of that kindness. I don't want to move. I don't want comfort. I have only one desire, and I know too well it's out of my grasp.

Petrarch didn't have to come. There are many demands on his time. He's as famous today as Father ever was. But I don't think Petrarch enjoys his fame as he used to. Like Father, he carries a weight of deepest sadness. He's felt the chill of that eternal winter, too. Which begs the question— can you only be a great artist if you have felt great suffering?

"I should become an artist, then."

"What was that?"

I shake my head. Petrarch tries to be patient with me, but it's not in his nature. "Pietro, time makes fools of us."

"It always does." Rising from the deep recess of my carved wooden chair, I step around the wing of my family. I've grown superstitious of late. Stepping on the wing might call the attention of angels. Or of Mercury, tasked to deliver messages and escort the dead.

Petrarch steps aside for me. Poor fellow. It is always sobering to see the wreck of a man you knew in his prime.

And I see my wreckage in Petrarch's eyes when he looks at me. I've shrunk this last month. Not eating anymore. Can't keep anything down. My hands ache. My shoulders are rounding forward. I've limped since I was seventeen, but I now have to lean on a stick to get around the whole vineyard for our daily walk.

Yet there's strength left yet in these legs of mine. Sixty-four years of life has not robbed me my freedom of movement. Or of thought.

They have only robbed me of everything else.

Sixty-four years. More than Father ever attained. Though by his reckoning he had only reached the halfway point of his life at thirty-five. By his count, I have six years left. It's cowardly to say, but I hope I don't.

Petrarch is younger than I am, and looks it. But then he never spent time as a knight, fighting in the field. I did, though it's many years since I lifted a blade or lance. The only sword I've wielded these last twenty-odd years has been the sword of Justice, dressed not in armour but in my judge's robes, riding not a horse but a bench. I show the signs of muscle gained and lost, leaving my arms fleshy and my belly a trifle pot-shaped. Whereas Petrarch has always been lean and always will be.

Yet in his limpid poet's eyes I see an echo of the same wreckage. He knows what I'm going through. He lost his child, too.

But that wasn't his fault. This is mine.

"Let's go."

Out in the yard, amidst the high green hedges, stands the lone lemon tree my Dolce planted. She'd been pregnant with our first child at the time, and it still makes me smile to think of her on her knees in the dirt, singing to our unborn daughter of the lemons that would grow alongside her. *Lemon tree, lemon tree, so pretty, smells sweet. Lemon tree, lemon tree, much too sour to eat.*

"Pretty day," said Petrarch.

"Yes." *Lemon tree, lemon tree, how much do you see? Lemon tree, lemon tree, I see that little bee.*

"Warm for September."

"Mm." *Lemon tree, lemon tree, are your lemons free? Lemon tree, lemon tree, no, they cost a fee.*

Lemon tree, lemon tree, what is your fee? Lemon tree, lemon tree, all that belongs to thee.

We're long past the tree, through the hedge arch, and walking along the hill's slope when Petrarch at last asks the question. "What does Morsicato say?"

"Soon. He says soon."

"He still won't let you see her?"

"She won't allow it."

"You sent for her husband?"

"No." My bitterness is evident. "I made that mistake once already. Better he comes when it's over."

"He won't like it."

"No. But he'll be alive. Betha's children won't be deprived of both parents."

We walk on a ways, coming to the rickety bridge over the stream. I stop to splash a little water on my face.

"She came for love of you."

"I know."

"Doesn't make it easier."

"No."

I feel grateful for his understanding. How terrible is that? What does that say about me? I'm grateful that my friend's son died last year, because he can comfort me now. Death has made monsters of us all.

We walk. Walk away from Death. Lord, but it's beautiful here. Rolling green, lush purple. Everywhere you look, life flourishes. I don't appreciate it often enough, how lucky I am to live here. I can look across the valley, the hills, the village, the vineyards. God's creation, in my keeping.

We've walked two miles and we're still on my land. Being rich isn't so much the joy of wealth, but the comfort of no longer being poor. The cares of money have gone. I was poor for so long, lived the stress of never knowing where the next meal would come from.

Now the poor come to me for help. They stumble into

the village and place their caps on the central fountain, pleading for aid, for food, for succor.

And we shun them. Because they might be carrying Death on their breath. We learned that lesson back in '48, when it first arrived. We took in the sick, because it was the Christian thing to do. We ended burying over half the village. Christian burials, for Christian charity. It seems a poor payment.

I survived then, just as I've survived this. So lucky. I've been lucky all my life. And, like a fool, I thought that luck would extend to my children. I see now, luck doesn't carry in the blood any more than poetry. I did not inherit my father's talent. My children did not inherit my luck.

What I did not understand until now was the high cost of luck. It's having to watch the luckless suffer.

I deserve to suffer.

Apropos of nothing, Petrarch says, "Back in '48 I wrote a letter to my brother. You remember him?"

"Of course." Gherardo had once almost challenged me to a duel, thinking I had gotten his sister with child. In fact, she'd been seduced by a churchman, which made Gherardo's eventual entrance to the monastic life all the more ironic. But then, the family had always had strong church ties. "I'm glad he survived."

"You'd think God would at least spare his own," retorts Petrarch. "Of thirty-five monks, he was the last one living. Him, and the monastery's dog. He had to bury them all. A surfeit of wormfood."

My stomach lurches at the thought of the grave I'm going to have to dig. Of my sweet Betha in the earth, food for worms. They're no longer making mass graves, thank God. Fourteen years ago, the bodies were piled so high in churchyards that there was no distinguishing between them. At least now the dead received proper burial. It's something.

I blink, remembering Petrarch had a point to make. "You said a letter?"

"Yes. I've been revising it of late. I wrote then that I

wished I'd never been born. Foolishness, of course. One can't help being born, though we cry at birth, as if we know what is to come. 'On all sides is sorrow. Everywhere is fear.'"

A bleak outlook. But then, the world was bleak today.

"I also wrote I wish I'd died before these times."

I sigh. "I wish that often. But the Lord has set His dictate against self-slaughter. So life must be endured. Why revisit the letter?"

"There's something in it. I mean, there was much that was raw. Of course. But it had strength. It was honest. I was hoping you would read it."

I refrain from groaning. Petrarch still thinks of me as the poet's aide. Just because I penned a companion to help people understand my father's work doesn't mean I enjoy poetry. Especially poetry about Death. Especially now.

Aloud I say, "Of course I will." The weight of obligation.

He claps me on the back in thanks, then resumes walking. As he walks, he talks, as if I've invited him to hold forth. It isn't welcome.

"At one point I observe that it's as though time has sped up, and we're forced to move in a frozen motion along the ground as others race by in headlong flight. Like mayflies, they're born, live, and perish so rapidly, while I trudge through my life at the pace of a snail's baggage train. I feel like an observer to nature, watching dying throngs of both young and old, and nowhere is there a refuge. No haven beckons in any part of the globe, nor can any salvation be seen. Wherever I turn my frightened eyes, their gaze is pummeled by continual funerals. Churches groan under the encumbering weight of biers as, without even last respects, noble and common corpses lie in confused equality alongside each other."

That's the trouble of befriending poets. Their love of words forces them to express their every thought. Even if the timing is less than ideal.

He carries on. "I've spent a great deal of time thinking about posterity. How future generations will be unable to believe that, without fire from heaven or fire from earth, without wars or rapine or the slaughter of steel, that the earth has been denuded of humans so thoroughly. When has such a thing been heard of? We read of Sodom and Gomorrah, of Pompeii and Herculaneum, of Atlantis sinking beneath the waves. But all of those, every one, was localized, with a specific cause for its devastating effect. Where in the annals of history has such a universal blight been recorded? Houses vacant, cities deserted, the countryside neglected, fields that should be plowed for food instead sowed with the dead. Our world today contains a fearful and universal solitude. How will anyone in the future believe it?"

"The same way we view history," I say. "With indifference. With a remote kind of pity. With a certainty that it couldn't happen today."

Petrarch shook his head. "I fear they'll think we deserve it."

My brows clench like a fist. After weeks of sorrow and despair, I'm almost grateful to feel the fiery tornado of anger that billows up from the pit of my stomach and forces my mouth to open. "Are you saying my daughter —?!"

"Of course not! No more than Giovanni, or my beloved Laura, or your Dolce!" His anger is as hot as mine, and has been banked longer. "I mean all of us! Mankind! The sinful fruit of Adam's tree. Our descendants will look on our corruption, our depravity, and say we brought this on ourselves." I stare at him for a time, and he yanks the correct interpretation from my gaze. "You disagree that Mankind deserves punishment?"

"If you're asking do I think us sinful, of course I do. Do I think us more sinful than those that came before us? I do not. History records deeds that make me blench. We are more enlightened today than ever before. Are we perfect? No. Can we be better? Yes. Did we deserve this more than our ancestors? Resoundingly, I say no!"

Petrarch's mouth curls, just a little, just at the corners,

and I realize I've been goaded. The bastard. I can't argue that the flood of anger has given me strength. But I resent being manipulated. "Though," I add, "God may be punishing you for those ridiculous shoes you used to wear."

Petrarch actually chuckles. "My genitalia shoes? That's what the Pope called them. I will confess, they were more for display than comfort. If I were to endure one of your father's poetic revenges, I imagine I'd be forced to wear them across a road of nails."

"Or have them replace your actual genitalia," I supply.

Petrarch's eyes widen as he considers that horror. "Who's to say that our forebears didn't also wear penis shoes? Or that our descendants won't think of clothing even more ridiculous and offensive?"

"They couldn't possibly," I say, amusement throbbing around my eyes.

I check myself. At this very moment, Elizabetha, my child, my firstborn, is in my home, dying. What right do I have to laugh while she lies in agony?

I shudder, ending the brief relief. For a moment, I hadn't thought of her pain. What kind of father forgets his daughter's agony?

It's my fault. All my fault.

Two months ago, I turned away a sickly traveler. A woman, with the marks of the Death clear upon her skin, the smell wafting the air around her. We gave her food, but no bed. Told her to move along. She begged. We refused.

So she went to the local nunnery. The very nunnery where my youngest daughter, Antonia, was visiting my middle daughter, Alighiera, who had just taken holy orders just like her sister's namesake. Antonia was so sweet. So young. Just married to an Uberti, she had her whole life ahead of her. At twenty-four, she was like me at my knighting. Invulnerable. She had survived the Death when it first ravaged the land, so I suppose she imagined herself impervious to it.

Hearing I had turned the sick woman off, she had stayed at the nunnery to tend the woman. It murders my heart to think she was disappointed in me. Antonia felt obligated to help because I had refused. That knowledge haunts my bones.

The moment Antonia showed signs of the illness, I brought her home. The sick woman as well. It wasn't only guilt, but selfishness and fear. I wanted to preserve Alighiera. As Petrarch's brother knew too well, monasteries and convents were breeding grounds for the disease, the worst kind of irony. Petrarch had said it. *You'd think God would at least spare His own.*

I also wanted to punish myself. I had turned the sick woman away, and God was punishing me through my child. That was the part that made me rail at God. *I* deserved to suffer, not my Antonia. God should have spared her this, and punished me instead.

Cesco would have called me a fool. I remember him once challenging Church doctrine, mocking the notion that suffering ennobles. I'll say now that I agree with him. There is nothing noble in suffering. I certainly don't feel noble. Especially after what happened next.

I wrote to the rest of the family, my scattered children, pursuing their lives and loves, all in the very tide of their lives. Whereas their father is in the ebb. They write me more often since the death of their mother. But I was lucky. I was married to her for twenty-six incredible years. We had so many beautiful children together.

I am so lucky.

Receiving my news about her little sister, Elizabetha didn't even bother to write. No, my firstborn simply packed her bags and ordered a carriage from Florence. She'd stubbornly reclaimed her grandfather's position there, marrying Rustichino Obriachi and becoming a vital part of the city's nobility.

Would to God she had stayed there.

But no. She'd come to comfort me and look after her

sister. She was here, holding hands with Alighiera, when we buried Antonia. She'd held me while I wept, wept as I hadn't since–well, since Cesco, I suppose. Not even Dolce's death had wrecked me as my little Antonia's did. Betha held me as she would one of her children as I poured out my heart through my eyes. She assuaged my grief, talked me through the worst hour of it. She told me stories I'd never heard from their childhood. She made me laugh, even. She brought joy back to the memory of my lost child. Betha had saved me that night.

Next morning, she'd found the sores.

We walk on. More to fill the silence than from any real desire for conversation, I say, "I've been thinking about my knighting."

"That's it, rub that salt," jokes Petrarch, who's never received a knighthood.

"Well, it's not as if you've done anything worth recognition." He elbows me in the arm, and I carry on. "I received many gifts from–from my patron." Even after all these years, it's hard to say his name. "One of them was a book. You know the kind of thing. Universal knowledge, a variety of subjects..." I waved my free hand absently.

"Yes, yes." Petrarch rolls his eyes for emphasis. "Skimming the surface of all things, plumbing the depths of none. It is a statement on education today. A man should be forced to learn one thing, and learn it well."

"Yes. My father used to say it didn't matter what a man learned, so long as he learned to learn."

"Exactly!" My friend nods, approving. "Learn to learn, deeply. Once you know *how* to learn, you can learn anything."

It's a good conversation starter. But I don't want to be shunted off onto a side path. "Part of it was an *ars moriendi. 'The Art of Dying'.*"

Petrarch lapses into silence. Such books were of a

sudden very popular, during these, the *anni di dolore*. The years of suffering.

"Have you heard the latest fad in Florence?" he asks. "They're burning ox horn and sulphur in the market squares."

My nose wrinkles at the thought. "I can't imagine it works."

"Only so far as to cause sparrows to fall dead from the rooftops," laughs Petrarch darkly. "So, did it say anything memorable, this book?"

"One section listed the five temptations of the dying."

Petrarch snorted. "Was 'not dying' one of them?"

"Strangely, no."

We crest a hill and pause to look at the Lago di Garda, the sun's rippled reflection assaulting our eyes.

"The sins?" prompts Petrarch.

"Lack of faith to start."

"Seems reasonable. Though in all my years holding one Church position after another, I've never found demanding answers of God to do much good."

"Next, despair."

"Yes." It's all Petrarch can say to that. "And after?"

"Impatience."

"'For the love of God, end the suffering.' Absolutely. And then?"

"Spiritual pride, followed by avarice."

"Hm. Avarice is easy enough to understand. 'I earned this money, and I mean to be buried with it!' But a temptation of spiritual pride? Did they mean exalting one's self beyond one's station?"

"Yes. Like the Pharisees, who thought themselves better than their fellow Jews. Or the gentile Christians who thought themselves better than Jewish converts. Paul has a diatribe against them, telling them they're branches, not the root. 'Where pride reigns, God chastens,' they say."

"'Pride wants to grow where the best gifts are given,'" counters Petrarch. "After all, it's pride that caused Lucifer to fall."

"So is it our pride that caused this? Mankind's pride?"

I think about it for a time. I think of a child I once raised, a child not of my flesh but of my heart. The little Mercury. He saw religion as a danger, not a salvation. He recognized the corruption of Man extended to a church run by men.

Yet he had never ceased to believe in God. "I think–I think it's the arrogance of Man to think he can understand God's will."

"Spiritual pride," says Petrarch slowly.

"Yes. I think we try to assume blame, find causation in our behavior, to take control of the thing. Because there is nothing more terrifying than not being in control. Than thinking there was nothing we can do to stave off this blight, or the next. So we bargain and cajole and assign blame, all in the mistaken belief that we have power here. We do not. We are the victims of the stars." I laugh, though it comes out choked. "Cesco used to say that Man's greatest fear was that God's plan was not about us after all. He suggested that perhaps God was interested in bees, who lead much more orderly lives."

Petrarch stares at me. "You haven't mentioned Cesco in years."

"Shame on me. Maybe I do now because–this is what I felt back then, at the end. Only then, I had the power to change things. I don't know which is worse–having the power and failing, or having no power at all. The one is bitter. The other is utterly devoid of hope." I loose a hard smile. "Cesco once called himself "Fortune's fool.' His friend Romeo, too. Both of them, cheated of happiness by their stars."

Mention of Romeo prompts Petrarch's thoughts. "How is Mariotto?"

"Well enough," I say. "Lonely, I think. He keeps busy. Visits often. He came to Antonia's funeral. Antony, too."

"Are they still—?"

"It will never be what it was. How can it? But they make a point to dine together once a week. More out of duty than joy. They swore an oath, and damned if they're not going to keep it." I swallow, and it sticks in my throat. "For the sake of their lost children. Something we all share now."

Nodding, Petrarch starts ticking off the list on his fingers. "Lack of faith. Despair. Impatience. Spiritual pride. Avarice. It strikes me," he says slowly, "that those might as well apply to the mourner as the mourned."

"I was thinking the same."

He puts a hand on my shoulder. "It's not fair."

I want to shout at him. *Of course it's not fair! What does life have to do with fairness!?!* But, as ever, I recall that he knows what I'm going through. Even though Giovanni was born on the wrong side of the sheets, he was still Petrarch's beloved son. He only has one child left to him, Francesca. Whereas I soon will have six. Six, out of eight. So lucky. Just as I am so lucky not to have contracted the disease, when I held both my sick children in my arms.

I'm so damned lucky. Fortune's favourite. That's me.

We start the curve that will take us back to the house. "The worst part," I say, "is that I'm resentful."

"I'm sure."

"Not just of the disease. Of it happening again. I just endured one daughter's death. Couldn't God have spared me another?"

"I know it doesn't help, but she's at peace."

I bite back a retort. "I know."

We walk, the house looming closer. "Have you considered what you'll do next?"

I'm genuinely confused. "What?"

"You should take up a post somewhere. Be a judge."

"A judge?"

"The world is in need of a little law and order just now. Trade stagnates, businesses fail. There are too few workers, and no one wishes to be in the cities. Crime is now seen as the best way to raise funds. Tradesmen have abandoned their occupations to live lives of wild excess. After all, why not, when they will likely die tomorrow? We need order."

I shake my head. "I am not the man to give it."

"Aren't you the man who has always said the answer is always the law? That, in the law, all men may find redress, equality, and justice?"

"Not against God!"

"Of course not. But the world is lit only by fire today. Wouldn't it be better if the tapers were of justice rather than fearful license?"

"Petrarch," I say with weight. "I don't care about any of that. My daughter is dying."

"I know," replied Petrarch quietly. "But, if my experience can guide you, allow me to be your Virgil. The only way to avoid the chasm is to fill it. Trust me, it's true. There must be something to occupy you. After Laura, after Giovanni, I chose poetry. It is my profession. I'm only saying you might find comfort in yours."

I'm not certain I deserve comfort. But his words do penetrate my numbness. "The law," I say dully.

"The law," he agrees. "The place where you are not helpless. Where there is order, justice. Fairness."

"Fairness."

"Wouldn't it be good to make the world a fairer place?" He pauses, then adds, "She'll want to know you have a purpose."

And that's painfully true. Even on her deathbed, Betha will be worried for me, as her sister was. What have I ever done to deserve such love? How did I have such amazingly selfless children?

I am so lucky.

We arrive back at the house. Morsicato is waiting for me. His forked beard hasn't turned white so much as slate, the grey hairs looking like the bristles of the wire brush I have to scour my armour when it tarnishes up there on the wall.

I first met him nearly fifty years ago, and he'd seemed old to me. But then, at seventeen, everyone seems ancient. Closing in on ninety years, he's outlived everyone. But there's still a need for doctors, now more than ever. And he doesn't fear catching the disease. He won't even wear those masks other doctors do, the ones that look like beaks. Says they make his beard itch. Besides, he hates to look ridiculous.

"She's asking for you," he tells me.

It's time then. I should go. Instead I linger for a moment, gathering my will.

We're still a month away from peak lemon season, but I pluck an early lemon down from a branch and hold it loose in my hand as I start the ascent to my daughter's childhood room, which will also be her death chamber.

Lemon tree, lemon tree, so pretty, smells sweet.
Lemon tree, lemon tree, much too sour to eat.

There's a sweet smell in the air as I enter Betha's chamber. Incense, to cover the stench. We did the same for her sister. Smelling it now is like a punch to the gut, and I lift the lemon to my nose.

Betha is in the bed. Her arms are extended, as her armpits have swollen. That was how it started. Now her limbs carried the purplish spots that damned her as surely as an executioner's axe. Her eyes are sunken, and her skin looks slick with sweat. Yet she's lucid enough, when she sees me, to force a smile. She doesn't want this to be hard on me. As if it could be easy.

Taking the stool on her right side, I hold up the lemon. "I picked this for you." I hold it close, so she can smell it.

She closes her eyes, and for a moment her smile is genuine, if filled with regret. "Mother."

"Mother."

"I'll see her soon."

"Give her my love."

"What will you do, father?"

"I'm not certain."

She grips my hand. "Please, do not stay here, all alone in this empty house."

"No. No, I promise. I–last month someone mentioned they were looking for a judge in Treviso. I may accept that role."

"Good. Good." Her eyes are like deep bruises. She closes them to ease their burning pain. "Rustichino. You didn't send...?"

"No. After." After you're gone, my sweet.

"Good. The children. It will be hard. He's a good man, but he doesn't–he won't know..."

"They shall want for nothing," I say.

Her smile is so sad. "Except their mother."

"Except that."

We're quiet. I want to say something profound, but I have never been the one with the words.

I see her lips moving, and I lean close. She has no voice for it, but she's singing:

Lemon tree, lemon tree, how much do you see?
Lemon tree, lemon tree, I see that little bee.

Softly, I start to sing with her, the way her mother did:

Lemon tree, lemon tree, are your lemons free?
Lemon tree, lemon tree, no, they cost a fee.

We both weep as we sing:

Lemon tree, lemon tree, what is your fee?
Lemon tree, lemon tree, all that belongs to thee.

"All that belongs to thee," I repeat, stroking her hair.
I am so lucky.

Late at night, after Morsicato has pried my warm hand from her cold one, I return to my study. Petrarch is abed, but he has left a paper for me. His reworking of his old letter to his brother. There was something in it, he said. Absently, I pick it up and read:

Imagining the last hour of life, I'm obliged to recollect my misfortunes. I recall flocks of dear ones departed, and conversations of friends, sweet faces suddenly vanished, and hallowed ground now overburdened with repeated burials. This is what the people of Italy bemoan, weakened by so many deaths. This is what France laments, exhausted and stripped of inhabitants. The same goes for other peoples, under whatever skies they reside. Either it is the wrath of God, for certainly I would think that our misdeeds deserve it, or it is just the harsh assault of the stars in their perpetually changing conjunctions. This plague has borne down on humankind and threatens a tearful slaughter, and the highly charged air encourages death.

From his diseased heavenly pole, cruel Jupiter looks down, and from there he rains upon the earth diseases and grievous mortality. The merciless Fates rush to sever the threads of life all at once, if they can. Seeing so many ashen faces of the wretched common people, and so many seeking gloomy Tartarus, I fear that from on high they may have been granted what they wish.

Just thinking of these things, I confess I am frightened. I see before me the snares of imminent death. For where could I hide my head, when neither the sea nor the land nor the rocks full of dark caves show themselves to the one who flees, because death, rushing impetuously into even safe hiding-places, overcomes all things.

Thus, like the mariner caught in a dangerous storm, before whose eyes cruel Neptune has sucked down the other ships in the convoy, who hears the fragile keel cracking in the belly of his ship and the splintering of the oars as they are dashed against the reefs, and sees the rudder carried away amongst the terrifying waves, I hesitate, uncertain as to what to do, though certain of the peril. No differently, where unnoticed a deadly fire has taken hold of ancient timbers and greedy flame licks resin-rich floorboards, the household, aroused by the commotion, suddenly gets out of bed, and the father, before anyone else, rushes up to the top of the roof, gazing about him, and grasping his trembling son seeks to save him first from the dangerous fire, and works out in his mind how to escape with this burden through the opposing flames.

Often in fear, clasping to myself my helpless soul, I too wonder whether there is an escape-route to carry it out from the conflagration and I am minded to extinguish the bodily flames with the water of tears.

But the world holds me back. Headstrong desire draws me and I am bound ever more tightly by deadly knots. That is the state I am in. Dense shadows have covered me with fear. For whosoever thinks they can recall death and look upon the moment of their passing with fearless face is either mistaken or mad.

My eyes pooling, I take up a pen. Pausing over the words, I add just two lines:

Or, if fully aware, very courageous.
We should all be so lucky.

Inspiration of David Blixt's On All Our Houses

It's strange to write an epilogue to a tale you're only halfway through telling. But ever since I started *The Master of Verona* in 2000, I've struggled to find a proper way to close out Pietro's story. Despite the hell I put him through in my novels, he was quite real, and I've always wanted to visit him at the end of his life to see what he made of it.

He was very successful, and sadly I'm sure that part of his success was due to the Black Death. How much land was there for sale, thanks to the plague? If one was already fairly well off, how much more money could be made when one third of the population has simply been plowed under?

His friendship with Petrarch was very real. It was tempting, I'll admit, to add Bocaccio to the mix, and recreate his setting for *The Decameron* in Pietro's house. After all, that story is set in a villa with people sharing tales while escaping the Black Death in the cities. In the end, however, I opted against that, because it felt like I'd be using the death of Pietro's daughters for a story that wasn't focused on him and his. The losses were quite real, and so deserve the weight of narrative and not to be cast aside for the sake of symmetry.

Much of Petrarch's cogitations on the Black Death come from that (real) letter to his brother, written to console the sole survivor of that monastery's infection. Petrarch had indeed lost his only son the year before. It was a horrible time. One can barely conceive the scope. The only parallel in my lifetime was growing up during the late 80s and early 90s, when adults I knew from theatre were suddenly dying from AIDS. Because it was horribly shamed, the grieving was considered less acceptable and therefore kept entirely private. The loss of my dear friend Rick Hunt was particularly shocking, as he hadn't told anyone that he was ill. As I thought of Rick, Petrarch's thoughts on what future generations would think hit me very hard.

Pietro himself died less than two years after this story takes place. What is truly odd, at least from my perspective, is that he died on April 21, which is also my wedding anniversary. It's a date that keeps cropping up in my writing, as well as in my life.

Pietro still had his other children, and they visited him and kept his line alive, right down to the present day. I've had the great honour of visiting the very same house that Pietro built in the Valpolicella region, staying as a guest of the Count Serego Alighieri, Pietro's direct descendant. I've slept in that house, lived in those rooms, walked through those vineyards. I know the path Pietro walks in this, because I walked it myself, in much happier circumstances.

But this is not a story of happiness. It is a tale of

endurance. As the song from *Hamilton* notes, the loss of a child is unimaginable. Yet all too real for far too many. My heart breaks for the unknown daughter, whose life ended needlessly, and far too soon. Farewell, *mo chidrhe, cuore mio, mi corazón.*

Farewell, my heart.

Learn more about David Blixt at https://www.davidblixt.com

A Certain Shade of Red

By Jean Gill

Venezia
August 1576

I'm not supposed to have favourites. Or to feel anything. Yet, I watch this man sweat and thrash about on his stinking bed and I wonder whether I will offer him one last gift. I know what he hopes and what he fears, even now. We have history together. The Dolomite mountains watch us through the north-facing window of his workshop. They are misty-eyed with summer but they remain stone, as they should be. I am neither misty-eyed nor stone.

I'm not supposed to dance, either, but you'll see me portrayed everywhere, whirling the human chain in a hop-skip *ballo* that links lady with leper, tinker with trollop, doge with dullard in the final music. Everyone dances in the end, holding hands—or what remains of them. Some call me the Great Leveller. You know who I am.

I do not need to intervene to promote pestilence. I did not cancel the embargo on contact from plague-ravished Verona. The city fathers chose between strangling Venezia's trade and inviting black buboes to the city. The choice was a foregone conclusion. After all, more of the rich fall from black trade days than from buboes.

I did not drain canals to prevent the foul miasma of yellow summer. That was a suggestion from the Health Office. Nobody realised that there would be fewer ways to transport the piles of rotting corpses out of Venezia, La Serenissima. Not so serene now.

I do not draw crosses on plague-house doors with the victims' blood. That is doctors' work when they confirm the presence of God's curse.

I just observe until my moment comes.

I observe now. Through the window, the mountains look blue and distant, as they appear so often in his work, a backdrop to human drama, a vision of something beyond pain and joy, a calm beyond judgement. These mountains are where he's from: Pelmo, nicknamed "the Doge's hat," and jagged Marmarole, that he could see from his childhood home. He wants to go home when his time comes. Not for his body, living or dead, to take a last journey to the new hospital, Lazaretto Nuovo on the *quarantino* island, rowed by country boys or felons. These are the only men willing to do such work, even for one hundred ducats, to be paid by the canny senate when the plague is over.

Even now, the *medico per la terra*, known as the body-check doctor, is on his way to this house from the Health Office building on the Piazza San Marco. Doctor Paragatto has been informed of sickness here and his job is to check the sick and the dead, to pronounce sentence and consequence.

"Are you there?" He speaks and strains to raise his head, peering with half-blind eyes. He is very old: one hundred and three, his obituary will say. His obituary will say much that is false, with the best of intentions. But it is not yet written and I could change it. There is precedent. Interventions have been made.

"Are you there?" the man asks again and I cannot help myself.

I answer, "Always. I have always sat for you. Don't you remember?"

He does not hear me. He is calling Orazio, his favourite son, his heir. "Orazio," his voice quavers, breaking. Orazio is out, seeking oranges in the market, and does not come.

"Please God," prays the man in the bed, in the faintest of whispers, a last effort, "spare Orazio from this pestilence." Yes, that is one of his fears. He too knows that the doctor is on his way.

As always, the doctor resents that he has to pay a boatman from his own purse, but today a bigger grievance against his employers hangs over him like the corrupt air over the gilded domes of the city.

There are always gondolas for hire, moored by the *piazzetta*, innocent in daytime. Venezia deals with her plague victims by night. He rejects a gondola with a new-fangled box for a simple one. He has no desire to be cooped up and he dreads the thought of darkness with the sound of water around him. As he visits the sick daily, he sees no point in paying extra to have wooden boards between his nose and the Laguna vapours. He slumps onto the bench, swears silently at the Doge's Palace as it swims graciously past, mocking him with its stone mouths and pretty façade. He chokes on bitter complaints that will never be voiced, and never be swallowed.

He passes the new round-bottomed ships at the entry to the Arsenale shipyards. There are many ways to die, and wars against the Turk compete with pestilence for numbers. Shipbuilding continues, behind the locked gate and the double tower, guarded by San Marco's lions. The saints' protection is in great demand and therefore, as befits a great trading city, supply of holy remains has increased. San Rocco's numerous finger-bones are the most popular relics now, may he protect them all from plague.

This doctor puts his faith in more earthly solutions. He understands that purifying a body from sin will prevent corrupt exhalations from making a cycle of pestilence, but his precious cure breaks that cycle in the physical world. He takes cold, dry herbs as a preventative against plague's wet heat.

By the time the doctor has landed on the Fondamenta Nuova, I will have made my decision about the man in the bed. And my decisions are always final.

I take his hand, almost as bony as mine now, and dance him back through time to where he stands in front of his easel, a rich man's gut overhanging his breeches. His constant petitions for payment have been rewarded this year.

Ingredients for the painter's alchemy surround Tician, an artist in his prime. Fresco plaster, panels and canvases in every type and stage: twilled and herring-bone, fine and heavy; some stretched on sized supports, virgin; some colour-blocked or fully painted with elements still wet, being re-worked. Brushes and lamp oil for cleaning them.

And the pigments! "A good painter needs only red, white and black," Tician says, and there they are in a hundred variations and mixtures. The Venetian essentials: white lead, coal black, and surely the best collection of reds in Venezia, from plants, insects, clay, lead, and minerals. Red lake from the madder plant, carmine from the cochineal insect, vermilion from cinnabar, and, of course, Venetian red, *ocra rossa*, from the ochre shipped from Turkey to this port of many secrets, an earthy shade of scarlet. Despite his pronouncement, Tician does not disdain the luxury of gold, or lapis lazuli. He cannot blame his pigments for the days he hates his work and changes everything he'd fixed the day before.

His assistants avoid disturbing the master as they complete their assignments, some elevated to the work of copying or filling in areas of worked canvas. Others grind pigments, a constant whirr over which Tician's friend, Pietro Aretino, raises his voice, with the ease of habit.

"Must you wear clothes, Angela?" complains Aretino. He waves his maimed right hand at the lady who flirts with her reflection in the mirror. A rather fine mirror, of *cristallo* glass from Murano, reflects a green satin gown, with pearl-embroidered borders and matching pearl buttons, demurely fastened over a loose cream chemise. Angela smooths her rippling hair, golden threads gleaming like the satin. One cream sleeve falls back, revealing pearly skin. She leans towards the mirror and her throat stretches, circled by a fashionable paternoster necklace, a pearl rosary for kissing. Men who worship at the altar of Zaffeta, as Angela is known professionally, rarely lose their faith. Among such men is Tician's customer, a cardinal, who wants to own a painting of the naked woman he can only hire per hour. Nobody buys Angela.

Losing interest in her reflection, Angela slips out of the green gown, drops the chemise from her shoulders and laughs. "I thought you sought novelty!" Despite the laughter, all present know that this painting does not just break with tradition. It smashes propriety into *cristallo* smithereens. A woman, bold and naked, in oils on canvas.

Tician frowns at her as his assistant rescues the expensive props from where the lady dropped them. The gown and golden ball are returned to their chest. He appreciates Angela but he does not love her, not in that way. Her rippling hair, loosed, is too yellow.

She favours him with her playful mind, not with her professional talents as, so rumour says, Venezia's second-most expensive courtesan. Aretino might be right. He believes that *she* started this rumour and now pretends irritation. There is no doubt who made public Zaffeta's orgasmic honesty. The only whore in Venezia who doesn't feign pleasure. As Aretino points out, the beauty of such a claim is that nobody capable of doing so is motivated to prove otherwise, and her competitors are confused into silence.

Aretino turns serious, with good cause. "I must seek novelty in a pastoral setting, *mia cucciola*. The complaint against me this time is formal and I must leave society until it is forgotten."

No need to ask what accusation has been lodged against a man who dips his pen daily in blasphemy and titillation, writing from his own vaunted experience. He has only escaped a public end, strung between the pillars of San Marco and San Theodore, because he is so useful to the Republic. He has escaped such an end so far, at least. And even the Council of Ten could be shocked into action, however much Aretino insists that the vile acts he describes took place in Rome, and how lucky Venetians are to be protected by their wise governors. Aretino is also known as a master of satire and absence would certainly plead his cause more effectively than any speech. Even he calls his pen "plague-ridden."

"*Mia cucciola*," murmurs Tician, his voice a caress, but he is not talking to Angela. A tawny spaniel weaves around her master's feet, another kind of discarded prop.

"How bland our lives will be without you to spice them!" Angela speaks to Aretino but gazes at Tician, as is required. She has taken up the previous day's reclining pose on red cushions, and is now wearing only pearl-drop earrings, a bracelet, a ring and her loosed fall of golden hair. Her angled head, heavy-lidded eyes, straight patrician nose, and pure mouth could belong to any chaperoned girl glimpsed across a palace ballroom. One demure braid still circles her head, formal as the earring. Not even her finely plucked and arched eyebrows or the extra redness of that lightly closed mouth would cause worry in a noble father. But he would turn white at the way her hair spills loose over her naked body. She shows no shame at such looseness. It is not only Aretino who knows the tricks of titillation, who knows how to shock.

"Put your hand… there." Tician places Angela's left hand in a delicate curl, the ring showing to advantage.

"How classical," she observes. "*Pudor et pudenda*."

"How interesting," says Aretino, a light in his eye.

Tician's Latin is poor, but he understands them both, modesty and pleasure. This is exactly what he wants, this ambiguity in the gesture. He is lost in the beauty of this gesture and does not care what others call it.

Angela frowns, shrugs her right shoulder. "My other arm feels clumsy, unnatural."

It would not be the first time Tician has to change a limb, or a head, or even a full person, on a finished canvas. He envies his fellows, so sure of themselves, while he works and reworks, doubts himself, throws white lead paint onto the offending element. From his fresco work, he is accustomed to waiting out the *giornata*, the time paint takes to dry.

He paces, goes to the window for inspiration, looks at his garden without seeing the roses, slightly blown now. Roses in Venetian red. "Maybe..." he says and gives orders.

When the assistant returns, Tician gives Angela a posy to hold so that her right hand echoes her left, one flower dropped on the matching cushions.

She is pleased. "Symbolic," she says.

"Interesting," says Aretino.

"Balanced," grunts Tician.

They are distracting him now, with their talk. He wants to work, to rework yesterday's mistakes, to grab pigment in his hand and smear it on canvas, to run his nails over textures, to throw passion into colour. But he must be patient. He must mix lead white with red lake to get pale rose. Layer upon layer, transparent on opaque, or vice versa, is the technique for which he is told he offends nature. His work is so much better than nature's. Layer upon layer is his technique but not his secret. Technique can be copied.

"I must go," says Aretino, his eyes still on Angela, his voice husky. "When I return, I will follow up on my suit to be cardinal." Nobody thinks this an odd choice of profession.

Tician thinks of his customer, also Zafetta's customer, already a cardinal, Ippolito de' Medici. "Your cardinal will hide this away, his private sin."

"Criminal!" was Aretino's verdict while Angela's gaze remained as serene as that of her painted image. "You *must* invite your patrons to see it first! Every man will want her!"

"And if they do," mused Tician, because he knew they already did, and they would. "If they do, I shall expand my workshop, hire more assistants. They can make copies, do the basics on my paintings." He remembers himself as a boy, learning the basics.

"Not just copies, make series! The same painting, with

different detail, here or there. Put the dog in one, for fidelity! You'll make a fortune!" With that parting encouragement, Aretino left.

"What exactly did my cardinal commission for this painting?" asked Angela.

Titian grinned. "You. Naked."

"Subtlety might further your plans better," suggested Angela. "Have you considered the heroines of classical myth? How beautiful they were? How morally acceptable their stories are? Even a classical title lends grace to a painting."

He considered them: Europa, Leda, Danae, Diana. All respectable subjects and all, in his imagination, naked and beautiful, with flowing red hair. Even clothed, such subjects could be sensual.

He returns to his easel. He will redden the hair more, let its silky ripples pick up the tones of the flushed nipples. This is no longer Angela but Beauty itself, always in the same form, always demanding his fidelity, in whatever woman Beauty currently resides. He knows when he sees her that she has come once more into his life.

He remembers the first time, Cecilia. Why, he wonders, was he so reluctant to marry her? Her hair was longer, wilder, silkier than Angela's, and a certain shade of red. His heart leaps. He knows the colour of his heart because it always seeks its twin.

I allow Tician's longing to pull me and my dancers with him to a different studio, an earlier time but the same accessories and smells. Linseed and walnut oils; gums, varnishes and resins; primed canvases drying; a heady mix. His palette of reds and creams is mixed from pigments he buys from the dye-seller. His favourite *vendicolori* supplies dyes for both fabrics and artworks, from his shop in the Rialto. Tician tries to match the pigment of his painted fabric to that used in the original dye, but he prides himself on enhancing texture, colour, and quality.

Another woman poses with her chemise dropped, this time enough to tease but not reveal her rosy nipples. Her mouth and oval face could belong to Angela's sister, but the eyes glance away, pensive. She glows, the silken cream of her chemise drapes the barely perceptible swell of her belly. Cecilia in all her sweet bloom, holding a posy of roses. Without artifice, without frizz, her hair flows from its straight, puritanical parting in the ripples left from unbraiding. The waves are tighter where the braids were thinner, reflect more gold. Titian loses himself in light, shade and layers, in loosened hair.

"It will be a boy," he tells her. His mouth turns down in concentration, in repose, making his smile irresistible.

She holds the exquisite pale rose velvet shawl in place with her peasant's hand. Tician creates texture in the shawl as carefully as he smooths the pearly flesh into perfection. He feels the same prickling gooseflesh on his own skin as when he signed a receipt Tician *Pittore*, "the Painter," for the first time. His apprenticeship is finished.

"You said you would marry me," she says, without accusation. They have lived together for years. It is true. He did promise marriage when he seduced her from the village he still calls his home. Her barber father still shaves his customers beside the sawmills where Tician's men shave wood. Larch, fir, birch, and alder travel by river and sea, to form lashed rafts by the Zattere, a steady income. Like the wood, Cecilia belongs to him, has travelled from his homeland, and she smells of forests, not of musk. She would pack cheese in a knapsack for him, for his son.

"I will," he tells her. "But not yet. We have no need to rush."

It will be a son but not always a blessing. It will take two sons and a desperate malady for Tician to make a wife of Cecilia, but she is not unhappy. She knows that he does not keep whores, as his friends do, but merely paints them. She does not know that he is passionately in love with Beauty, and a certain shade of red, which will abandon Cecilia.

I pull him back into the dance.

"Tician!" calls a voice. This is his name in Venezia. Exhausted from the journey of four days, jostled to bone on raw buttocks, the boy nevertheless gasps as he steps onto the quayside, in the grand shadow of the wooden bridge famed as the Rialto.

If this is land, he knows of no land like this, shimmers of shabby gold palaces echoing to the skies what the boy saw in the water. He'd dipped his hand in the canal, to make the palaces quiver, but withdrew it quickly when he saw the contents of a chamber-pot splash nearby.

He spots a face like enough to his father's hooked nose and fierce glare, for him to reach out, but he is nine years old, a big boy now. He doesn't need his uncle's frown to let the hand drop back down, wiping it on his breeches, remembering where it's been. Venezia lays claim to her newest citizen.

"I saw four hundred flowers on the way here and I will paint them all," he tells his uncle, who ignores him.

"Come along then," orders his uncle, without offering to take the small knapsack packed so carefully by Tician's mother. The boy hefts his burden, still smelling of mountain cheese, and fights tears by observing the marvels around him as he trots in his uncle's wake, another road he must travel.

Market stalls are the least strange—until the boy sees the outlandish goods displayed on them: living creatures squabble amongst musical instruments. He doesn't know which are pets and which are food but assumes that a marmoset sitting on a shoulder is the former and a rabbit is the latter. Fine fabrics are unrolled and furniture repaired.

He recognises some vegetables and knows the word "spice" but has never seen or smelled the variety on offer. And as for the fish! He knows trout and eels, even pike, whatever can be caught from rivers, but these stalls are crawling with live crabs and tentacles, slithery with ugly-mouthed sea-fish big enough to feed his whole family.

A shout from behind attracts Tician's attention. "Sold! Forty ducats! To the gentleman in blue!" He looks back and sees a woman freed from chains and pushed towards a man in a blue doublet.

Men with fancy earrings and quilted jackets offer riches to those willing to play just one game of cards at their tables. Tician does not know how to play cards. He will ask his uncle as that seems a less tiring way to become rich than in a painter's workshop. And Tician is very tired.

Then he sees the women! His mouth gapes as his eyes catalogue these chirruping birds of passage; blonde hair, faces shaped into permanent surprise, gowns that begin below the shoulders, exposing red or even gilded nipples. The boy blushes, looks down at the ladies' feet, clipping along on high platformed clogs, in small, quick steps, as they pass him in a haze of musky scent.

His uncle laughs at the boy's embarrassment, points at a building, where a lady leans as far out of a window as out of her dress, calling mysterious obscenities. Tician knows they're obscenities because his father hit him for repeating one of them.

"When you're older," his uncle says, "if you work hard, you can call there and take your pick. Better to wait than risk the French disease somewhere cheap!"

Is that what he's working for? To take his pick of ladies? Will they pack good cheese and a change of clothes for him if he travels?

"I've had to call in some favours to get you an apprenticeship with Zuccato, so you'd better not let me down! He will teach you all the basics of art and then we'll see. What's considered fine in Cadore is ordinary in the grandest city in Europe, but you might even be an assistant one day. Aim high, my boy!"

Tician is only half-listening. He is all eyes. He sees porphyry and velvet, how light makes one hard and the other soft. Haggling and song come to him in pictures. Even the musk-scents of women turn into colours, tawny, amber, and rose. And so it begins for the Cadoran.

I drop the man's hand. He is a big boy now as he leaves the dance to follow his uncle and to fulfil his calling. I can return to the dance any time I choose, and summon any dancers but, for now, I have work to do in the sick-room, where a man's body lies empty on a bed.

Doctor Paragatto leaves the water slapping against his gondola, steadies himself and steps onto a level of stone that is dry but encrusted with water-weed from higher tides. He walks the back streets to the house of the famous artist, Tician. The Biri quarter is not fashionable, but the house itself has a large garden on three sides, in a city where greenery usually means the wrack left by the summer tide on the canal walls.

Pausing at the top of the steps from the garden to the upper rooms, the doctor admires the view. Even on such an errand, even with such resentment eating his liver, he cannot be unmoved by the vista across the Laguna to Murano, and beyond Murano to misty mountains. He can see why the Cadoran chose this house.

The Laguna shimmers and the doctor's duty settles on him again like a black pall. How can he admire the Laguna like an innocent? He is haunted by thousands of boats, traversing the sea at night like ill-omened moths. The white ones, which carry the sick to the *lazaretto* or, rarer, the quarantined back to the mainland; the black ones, which carry the plague dead for burial. If there are no white boats available, and the sick travel with the dead, driven to madness and death by their grim companions, is it his fault?

The senators average seventy-five years apiece and care more for budgets than for Health Office warnings. To their credit (and debit) they take care of the expenses for white boats and black boats alike. They are commissioning barges to carry the increased numbers of *poveri vergognosi*, the shame-faced poor, stricken by plague. The senators themselves and their ilk will always have gondolas, should such a ride be necessary.

Bile rises in the doctor's throat. Thanks to his wife and her father, he *knows* how to treat plague! He has taken the preventatives himself and here he is, living proof they work. He has stocked up on the correct variety of myrtle leaves and he has the leeches for blood-letting. He wrote to the senate a month ago, offering to sell Dr Colochi's secret cure to the plague, passed on to him in his wife's dowry.

He thought they'd rejected him, unwilling to even bargain over a payment. The Colochi cure is *worth* a large purse and a pension for life! Now, he's found out that the senate agrees with him—only *he's* not the one getting the money. His wife has a sister, who brought the same dowry to her husband, Paragatto's colleague and brother-in-law, who runs the *lazaretti*. No doubt the scoundrel used his position to run further tests on the cure, while Paragatto is tied to the regulations that protect the living! He knows that there are three patients to a bed in the *lazaretto* on the island, and so many corpses that a thousand more from testing cures will go unnoticed. He knows because it is his word that has populated the *lazaretto* beds and mass graves.

When he sees the corpse on the bed, the doctor is still thinking of his cheating father-in-law. Dr Niccolò Colochi passed on his precious secret to two daughters and their two husbands, leaving the more devious man to gain from it, like a true Venetian! Olivieri will be rich and lauded while he, Scipione Paragatto, is left with only 150 ducats per year and no allowance for expenses! The unfairness of it festers, a malady he cannot cure.

He pulls back the sheet but does not touch the corpse. If he can see plague symptoms, there is no need to investigate further. The man's tongue lolls black, not white, so that tells nothing. He has been sick but bile tells nothing. Those might be *carboni,* pustules with black centres, but Paragatto will need to look more closely to be sure of whether this death was caused by plague and he feels a strange reluctance to disturb this corpse. If he's not sure, then the death is suspect.

He opens his mouth to pronounce the sentence that cannot be rescinded. He knows the complicated regulations by heart, even to the reduced *quarantino* if only a downstairs servant has symptoms of the disease. But death by plague is clear-cut: the household is declared *suspetto di longa practica*. The plague cross will be marked on the door to Tician's house. The artist's possessions should be burned to destroy the miasmotic particles which cling to them but they could accompany him, be kept in *quarantino*. I remind the doctor of all this, add a tiny detail.

Dr Paragatto paces the apartment while he ponders. He goes into Tician's workshop, where he is blind to the view of the Laguna and distant mountains. All he sees are the paintings stacked against walls. One remains on the easel, a Pietà. Mary holds her son's white body in her arms conventionally enough, but Magdalena proclaims the passion of Christ, vibrant with grief that predicts her joy in the risen lord. Even a plague doctor can see that the master painted his soul into this unfinished work. There is even a likeness between the praying saint and the dead man on the bed, as he once was, bony face, hooked nose and fierce gaze. No cap hides his bald head here. There is honesty in contemplating Death in such a manner. What did Tician pray for when he painted his last work?

Unlike the doctor, I know the answer. You see, I was there. That was the last time I sat for the master, although I was never far from his studio. He contemplated Death many times, expressed himself in black and, of course, red. His final prayers were that he be laid to respectful rest in his home church, with his last painting, the Pietà. This is what he prays for, and for Orazio to be spared plague.

Surrounded by masterworks, the doctor sees instead his brother-in-law puffing up his chest as he boasts of the *lazaretto* being the last resting place of Venezia's most famous artist. "And these are his last works, his finest paintings," prestigious visitors will be told. Dr Paragatto knows this to be true. He is looking at them. "And I," Dr Olivieri will proclaim, showing his domain to these same visitors, perhaps the Council of Ten themselves, "I am the man who gave Colochi's cure to the city of Venezia. I am the man who saved this city." Will he even credit Colochi? Or will it be known as Olivieri's cure?

Dr Paragatto looks at the *Pietà*, imagines it in the *lazaretto*. Everybody has heard of the arguments about this painting, intended for Tician's last resting-place–one week that would be the church in his home village in Cadore, the next week, the grand Venetian church of the Frari. Never has one man dithered and haggled so much over his own memorial! Perhaps it would serve him right if he and his painting share an anonymous grave, among the thousands of dead, on that island which few leave. But then Olivieri would have Tician and his paintings, as well as credit for Olivieri's cure.

I share one more image with the good doctor and I wait. Signora Paragatto does not yet know that her sister and brother-in-law will be rich for life because of the secret her husband could not sell. He pictures himself telling her and comes to a decision.

Flushed, the doctor mutters to himself, "Symptoms ambiguous, no sign of plague." He does not look under the armpits, nor behind the ears so he does not have to lie, even to himself. The fever and death of an old man are hardly surprising, whoever he might be. Such a death need not become the responsibility of Dr Olivieri and his *lazaretto,* need not further profit that lucky colleague.

Dr Paragatto blows out his cheeks, notes the death as *non suspetto*, pronounces the household *libere* and leaves, clutching one little painting that will not be missed, a gift from a dying man, or so he will tell his wife.

In the marketplace, Orazio breaks out in a sweat and decides to return home straight away, without the oranges. He will have time to arrange what has to be a quiet, local funeral for his father. After all the disputes, which do not end with Tician's death, the Church of Santa Maria Gloriosa dei Frari will win Tician's tomb. One of his disciples will complete the *Pietà* in the style of the master.

It is not my place to comment on the divine response to prayers. My work is entirely practical and I am rather pleased with it. I have allowed myself a small intervention because I too am known for a certain shade of a red.

Inspiration of Jean Gill's A Certain Shade of Red

When I was given the opportunity to contribute to an anthology on the theme of the Black Death, I meant to say no because I was busy publishing two audiobooks and a boxset of *The Troubadours Quartet*. I was also starting the photography series I've waited a year for, working for a month in a forge here in Provence to shoot the making of a Damascene knife from raw metal to finished, polished artefact. However, the anthology was such an interesting idea, in the best company I could imagine! So I said yes.

The idea came straight away by association: plague–the famous Venetian doctor mask with its beak. I browsed online for historical inspiration, for a story set in plague-ridden Venice, and I found that Titian died of plague. I also found that Titian didn't die of plague. Then, that he probably died of plague but was not recorded as, or treated as, a plague victim. Curiouser and curiouser. Where there's a mystery, there's a story.

Then the research began. I was writing something completely new and different for me, about a period and place I'd not written about. I do know Venice well but I needed to do a lot of research, fast. Luckily, I love research and was willing to read large books, study paintings and read theses on medieval plague medication to write my little story. I already had background knowledge of medieval medicine from writing the twelfth-century *Troubadours* books, but by 1576 much of the earlier expertise in treatments had been lost. The year 1576 was a time of change. Thanks to the plague, a new era in medical theory and practice was beginning.

It helps to focus research when you know the date of your story, so 1576 was my starting point for all research. I discovered straight away that the Venetian plague doctor mask was not worn until the seventeenth century, and was in fact invented in France, although no doubt doctors covered their noses before that, and used posies of herbs. Good-bye to my atmospheric descriptions of the plague doctor's costume.

I was determined that my story would not be miserable, but how was that possible in a story about plague and mass death? My answer was to take the viewpoint of the only character for whom this is all in a day's work–Death. I very much enjoyed writing the sardonic, omniscient narrator.

While reading a treatise on plague medicine in Venice, I came across the Colochi cure and the true story of how one doctor son-in-law made his name, and a fortune, from selling this to the Senate. All the details I've included are drawn from reputable research. Only in Venice could you have such a story of inheritance, family secrets and rivalry, set in the paranoia induced by such a secretive state. Europe's best example of a gerontocracy, power in the hands of the oldest men, created a rich, complex setting for my story, full of ironies.

Why did I decide on Tician as the name for the artist we know as Titian, rather than his current label on Venetian monuments, Tiziano? I drew much of my information on Titian's life from Sheila Hale's book, *Titian: His Life and the Golden Age of Venice*. Titian signed his work and his invoices with several variations of his name and I liked the lesser known Venetian dialect version, to show that switch from "the Cadoran" (the man from Cadore) to being Venetian.

Why only mention one son and not Titian's other family, including much-loved daughters and grandchildren? A short story has to be focused and Orazio is Titian's personal and professional heir, Titian's hope for immortality. Doomed of course, as Death ironically observes. However, thanks to Death's "little intervention," and to Titian's many students, the flame is passed on to the next generation and to many after that. Next time I go to Venice, I will be looking out for "a certain shade of red" with the feeling I know the man famous for it.

My thanks go to all those who checked and improved my story, including two of my fellow-writers in this anthology. Without Kristin Gleeson, I would not have known that "pink" is such a modern word and was in fact a much-disputed colour. Laura Morelli's expertise on Venice and art history clarified a couple of points, such as how long paint really takes to dry–I grew bored watching it!

Titian's life story is fascinating and suggests so many spin-offs via other characters that I am still wondering about the women in his life, about whom so little is known. The two doctors deserve a novel to themselves as do his various friends and models. If only an author could write every story! For now, I am deep in a different fictional world, but maybe one day I will return to sixteenth-century Venice. I feel it calling me.

Learn more about Jean Gill at https://jeangill.com

The Repentant Thief

By Deborah Swift

Edenburg, Scotland
1645

Finn craned up at the dark hollow of the stone stairwell.
Nobody was about, so he set off leaping, two at a time, his
bare feet slapping on the flagstone stairs. *One two, cock-a-
doodle-do. Nine, ten, big fat hen.*

This tenement was his castle, and the narrow, shuttered
windows his battlements. At the top he stuck his nose out
of the broken shutter to take in the scrawl of smoke against
grey sky, the rain-slicked slate of the roofs, and the beetling
men scurrying below. Up here, he was a laird, just for a few
moments, or maybe a king.

He grinned. King Finn the First. Were there any kings
with fox-red hair like his? King of Ireland, he'd be, if they
ever went back home.

To ease the homesickness in his chest, he charged
downwards again, skidding breathlessly round the corners,
bouncing off the cold granite walls. Running up and down
stairs kept him warm, despite the lack of stockings on his
skinny legs, or shoes on his feet, or a warm cloak. He shot
along the landing, but paused mid-scoot and skidded to a
stop. A long puddle of light lay across the floor. Whooping,
he jumped into it with both feet.

A quick glance sideways. One of the doors was ajar, and
from inside came the muffled noise of a woman weeping.
Panting slightly, he peered through the gap to where a rare
sliver of Scottish sun shone through the chamber's open
casement windows.

Winter had been so bleak that the sunlight drew him.
Through the door the chamber spread out, lofty, light, and

so unlike his own home that it made his mouth fall open. The weeping had stopped now.

Just a quick deek, he thought. No one would know.

He nudged the door with a finger and it widened with a creak. A face stared out at him.

He exhaled. Only a painting. A portrait of a haughty woman in blue silk, whose eyes followed him as he stretched his toe inside, taut as a deer, ready to run. From the chamber behind, the weeping began again, and the soft murmur of another woman's voice.

They hadn't heard him. He crept a little further in as the sunlight pooled over a polished wood table and glinted on a scatter of gold.

One swipe, and something cold and hard was in his palm. Instantly, he was away, leaping helter-skelter down the stairs, flushed with victory and excitement.

A dour-faced man labouring upwards, a basket of coals strapped to his back, had to step aside. "Little rat! Watch yer step, can't you!"

But Finn didn't stop; he bolted out into the air, heart pumping. Grey cloud had shrouded the sun again, but around the corner, in the stink of fish near the wharf, he opened his palm to view his prize. A half-crown! And an oval of gold on a chain. He shoved the coin in his pocket, and turned over the other object.

A lass's trinket. And it could really be gold. He turned it over to see a tiny portrait covered by a bubble of glass. The locket was hinged so the picture could be changed under the glass. He prised it open with a nail and ran his finger over the curve of the glass, marvelling as he squinted at it, how the glass made his hand bigger. The crisscross of creases, the dark veins of dirt, the little wart on his thumb.

A gaggle of sailors lurched past him, and quick as a wink he closed his palm and sprinted past the rest of the tenements to the straggle of squatting cottages. The roof of his house was ragged. Ma said the burg had banned thatching, and his big brother Brendan had thought tiling it with wooden tiles was a good idea. The Edenburg winds had thought otherwise.

In through the front door and straight past Ma, who was weaving on the hand-loom in the middle of the chamber, his baby brother, Ruari, strapped to her back in a sling.

"Take a turn with the shuttle, won't you, whilst I feed Ruari?"

"Aw, Ma." Finn sidled past into the curtained alcove where the sleeping rolls were, and took out the locket again. Now it was here, he regretted taking it. It was the same woman as in the big portrait, he was sure of it. Was she the one weeping? She would miss it. Worse, that old man had seen him running down the stairs. He cursed his red hair, and wished he owned a cap. *Tinker, tailor, soldier, sailor, rich man, poor man...* King! He sighed. *Beggar man, thief.*

"Get yourself dressed," his father said, as Finn rubbed the sleep from his eyes.

"Whose turn for the cloak?" Brendan asked.

"Mine," Finn said, struggling to snatch the heavy folds from his grasp.

"You had it last time."

"Stop your fratch or I'll take it myself," Ma said. "Brendan, it's your turn. Finn had it last week."

Brendan slung the wool cloak around his shoulders and swaggered up and down. He was built like an ox, with ruddy hair to match, unlike his other brother, Patrick, who was thin as a weasel.

"It's too short," Finn said.

Brendan stuck out his tongue.

"Do we have to go to church?" Finn complained.

"Aye," Da said. "It's the law of the land. Even here."

"And ye can pray to the Lord God Almighty that he'll send your Da some work," Ma said. Finn dodged as she tried to flatten his hair.

He made a face and sighed. He missed the church at

home; the one with the pictures of devils and demons, and the waft of incense, and Father O'Halloran in his embroidered tablecloth and starched white ruff. The new kirk was like the rest of Scotland–damp, grey, and forbidding, with all the colour wrung out of it.

Father and mother walked ahead, with baby Ruari swaddled to Ma's chest, and the boys in a goosey gaggle behind; Brendan, Patrick, and Finn. Folk stared at their bare feet, at their patched clothes, at how thin they were. Nosey swine. Ma and Da paid no mind; they went silently, arm in arm, nodding politely to those they passed. They all filed into the very back row behind Angus, a cotter neighbour who always whiffed of liquor. Angus smiled toothily at Finn, releasing fumes of whisky, and a man in a steeple hat turned and threw them a cold, disapproving glare.

The craw-faced minister, Reverend Fett, arrived through a side door, bringing the cold with him. His grey skin bristled a pointy beard; his expression was dark as mutiny beneath heavy brows. His gaze raked the pews and settled on Finn's family with a down-turn of his mouth. He stepped onto the platform and began.

Immigrants, the minister said, were the scourge of Scotland. He spat out the word "immigrant" as if it were a louse. Immigrants had not embraced "The Covenant." Finn imagined some sort of invisible giant blanket over the land. But worse than immigrants were sinners. The minister prodded the Bible before him and listed them all.

Finn chanted the unfamiliar words in his head. *Adulterer, fornicator, usurer, whore. Counterfeiter, 'bezzler, harlot, thief.*

He felt in his pocket and the coin and locket slid cold and hard under his fingers.

"What did Our Lord send into Egypt against those sinners?" Reverend Fett asked. It wasn't a question anyone dared to answer. He thumped his fist on the lectern. "Plague and pestilence, fire and famine!"

There was a general unease; a shuffling and a lowering

of eyes.

"Who amongst you have sinned? Do you want to bring that upon your house? Or do you want to dwell in the House of the Lord forever?" He frowned, fixing Finn with a flinty eye. Finn recoiled and sat on his hands, his face burning despite the chill of the kirk.

He knew. Finn was sure of it. He had the uncomfortable sensation that Reverend Fett could see the stolen things through his clothes. Finn shrank down, picking at the fabric of his breeks where it was coming away from where it was patched.

"Stop fidgeting." Ma jabbed a sharp elbow in his ribs.

Once home, indignant voices rose up. None of them liked the minister. During the general cacophony, Finn slipped the coin out of his pocket and onto the table, glad to be rid of it. The locket he would have to keep. Someone might recognise it. Besides, you couldn't spend it. He'd have to get rid of it somehow.

It wasn't long before his mother spotted the coin. "What's a' this?" she said, waving it in the air.

A clamour as Brendan and Da went to look. "What is it?"

"Well blow me, if it's not a half-crown." She held it between finger and thumb with amazement.

"Where d'it come from?" Brendan asked.

"How should I know?" She rounded on them all. "I'll not have thieving in my house. You heard what the preacher said. God sees everything. And he'll punish those that disobey. Brendan?"

"Not me, Ma."

"Patrick?"

"Cross me heart an' hope to die."

"Finn?"

"I found it. On the street."

"Where?" Her eyes searched his face with that penetrating look that made him squirm.

"By the docks," he said. "I saw it glintin' and I picked it up."

She grabbed him by the arm. "If I find out you've lied, I'll skelp you, d'you hear?"

Finn swallowed and kept dumb. He'd always blarneyed it in Ireland and nothing ever happened. No great hand had ever reached out of the clouds to carry him off. Ma's attention was still on him, her lips pursed, and she was far more frightening than any invisible God.

He avoided her eyes. "I thought we could do wi' it. For the rent."

"Aye. That and a hundred other things. You sure it don't belong to anyone?"

"Told you. It was on the ground. Not a soul near."

"Well, you've sure got sharp eyes, our Finn, I'll say that for you."

"An' maybe it's the start of our luck," Brendan said. "Da's got a chance at the docks the morrow. They're looking for strong men, and Angus from the cottages has spoken for him; he told us on the way back."

The next day Da came home grinning and slapped his cap down on the table. "Wages on Friday!"

"What is it? What d'you get?" Brendan crowded into him, with Patrick after, tugging at his sleeve.

"Stevedore in Lyth. Start tomorrow. Two mile down the track to the docks, and I'm to unload timber from Norway."

Ma burst into tears. Da stepped from foot to foot. "Eh, dry those tears, Maveen. It's a wedding not a funeral."

"I know. It's just ... the relief. Finn needs shoes, and the roof needs more wood, and we could all do with a good dinner."

"Don't be spending it yet, wan." He swayed on his feet, then sat down at the table, and wiped his brow. His face was waxy and perspiring.

"You can't be sweating," Ma said. "It's cold as the Irish

Sea in here. Maybe we'll be able to afford coal now."

"It's the walk. It's knocked me flat."

"Tell us about the ships, Da." Finn leant an elbow on the table beside him.

"Not now, Finn. I have to be rested up for the morrow." Da heaved himself awkwardly to his feet and staggered in the direction of the bed alcove.

"You alright, Donal?" His ma hurried after.

"Leave me be, wan. I'll be right in the morning."

"I'll sleep out here with the babby then, in case he cries."

But that night, Finn heard Da tossing and turning in his bed and then the splatter of vomit as it hit the chamber pot.

"Da?" Finn crawled towards the roiling heap of bedclothes and put out a hand.

"Be gone with you." The words were slurred.

One too many, Finn thought. Best leave him then. He scrabbled back to bed.

When dawn came, his father's skin burned fiery hot and they could not get him up.

"Brendan, Patrick, go down the docks, tell Angus your Da's sick," Ma said. "He'll be there tomorrow. And Finn, find a physician," Ma reluctantly handed Finn the half-crown. "There goes our hot dinner." She sighed. "Look for the sign of the staff and snakes. We can't lose the chance o' work now. Tell the physick-man it's urgent. And for Jesus' sake don't drop that money."

Brendan and Patrick set off one way, and Finn pelted up the street the other way, into the oldest part of the town, up the narrow, squeezed alleys near the castle. He found the sign of the snakes, but a notice was nailed to the door and the shutters were battened down.

He hailed a passerby but she crossed the street to avoid him. Finally a wizened old man with a bent back approached the shop, and then tutted in frustration to find it shut.

"Please, sir, what does it say?"

"Gone away," he said. He jabbed a nail at the notice.

"Another yellow-livered coward fleeing when we need him most."

"My father's ailing," Finn said desperately. "Ma sent me to fetch someone."

"Sick, you say?" The man backed away, dragged a kerchief from his pocket and held it to his nose.

Finn stepped nearer. "Please, sir. I have money. He held out the coin on the flat of his hand."

"Get away," the man shouted.

Finn stood a moment, trembling as the man hurried away from him, stumbling down the steep wynd. Strange that so many shops were shuttered, he thought, as he scoured the streets. And some vagabond had painted crosses on all the doors. But one, an apothecary, was open. At the sign of the pestle and mortar, Finn burst in through the door.

The scant-haired man behind the counter eyed him with suspicion. "Keep your hands there on the counter where I can see them."

Finn put his hands palm down, and the half-crown slid out onto the dusty surface. The apothecary slapped it down and slid it into his pouch in one smooth movement. "What is it you're after?"

"Something for fever. My Da's not well. Ma sent me to get something."

"What's wrong with him?"

"A fever, and the vomits, and too much sweat."

The apothecary nodded, sucked his lips, moved away. "I've got what you need. Feverfew, vervain and chamomile. Never fails."

"Thank you, sir." He watched as the apothecary scooped dried herbs from a barrel.

"Where did you say you live?"

He hadn't, but the man was kind, so he answered him. "Bankside Cottages. Tail-end o' Burgh Street, beyond the tenements."

The man screwed the edge of the packet together and passed it over.

"Is there no change?" Finn asked.

"Ach, no, lad. They be rare herbs."

Finn was doubtful. It didn't look much, this flimsy packet, not for a whole half-crown. But the man made no move to give him anything back, so he bit his lip and turned to go.

"I wish your father well," the apothecary called.

Ma's face drew tight when he gave her the packet, and she sighed mightily, but brewed the herbs over the heat of a candle and Finn stood by the curtain whilst she fed the mulch to his father. He was much smaller lying down, and didn't look like Da at all. Brendan and Patrick came home with glum faces. Patrick had a big bruise across his cheek.

"What happened?" Ma asked.

"What do you think?" Brendan raised his shirt to show red weals and bruising. "It wasn't our fault. They set on us for no reason."

Ma shook her head. "Ye'll be the death of me."

"Let's have a deek at your ribs again," Finn said, "that big black bruise is the shape of Ireland."

Brendan shoved him away. "Leave off."

By the middle of the night Patrick was sick too, and the sound and smell of him made Finn clutch the straw pillow to his nose. The next morning Finn awoke to the sound of Ma bellowing like a horse in pain, and he jumped up from his pallet, tripping over Brendan's lanky legs in his hurry.

Ma stood away from his father's bed. Her hair hung round her face. She never had it loose; it was always tied up in a long plait under her coif. She hugged herself and rocked back and forth, back and forth.

Something bad was happening. Finn scrambled over to take hold of her skirt.

She put a hand on his head but did not speak.

His Da was still and his eyes were open in a dull stare. Finn reached out to try to wake him.

"Get away from him!" Ma shouted, suddenly animated.

"But—"

"Don't touch him! Get away, I said!" she dragged him back. Her shouting woke the others.

"What's all the noise?" Brendan asked.

"He's dead. Your father's dead."

"He can't be. He's just got—"

"No! Keep back." She grasped Brendan's arm. Patrick stood mute in the corner, white as whey, the sheet held up to his mouth.

A loud hammering at the door. They all shot guiltily upright, as if having a dead person in the house was something to be ashamed of. His mother tied a shawl around her hair and went to answer it.

Two big men filled the doorway with their bulk; one with a grey beard, one without.

The bearded one spoke. "We're from the Burgh Council. The apothecary told us a body's sick here."

"No one's sick." Ma tried to close the door.

"You sent your son to him for a remedy."

"You're mistaken."

Finn shrank back into the shadows, examining his bare feet. That these men were here, was somehow his fault.

The bearded man pressed Ma on the shoulder. "We must come in. Orders of the kirk elders."

"Who is it, Ma?" Brendan puffed out his chest. Patrick copied him, though he looked right poorly, and swayed on his feet. The two strangers bristled and put their hands to their swords, making Finn cower, his hands over his face.

Ma jumped between them. "Leave it, boys. Don't start with your trouble again." In an instant, she seemed to deflate, and the men pushed inside.

"Where's the sick man?" The clean-shaven stranger asked, waving a long white stick.

Ma's mouth quivered but she led the way and pulled back the curtain. The man poked his stick under the covers and lifted Da's shirt.

"Leave my da alone!" Finn yelled. It didn't seem right Da

should be prodded like that.

Both men stepped back as if they'd been stung and pressed kerchiefs to their noses.

"You know what this is?" Greybeard's voice was muffled under the wipe.

Ma nodded, but her eyes were leaking and her shoulders heaving. Finn went to hug her. It wasn't right, them barging in while she was grieving so.

"The cart will take your man to bury, and you will all be moved to Boroughmuir. Anyone who resists will be hanged. Am I clear?"

Boroughmuir. Finn heard it as "Borrow more." Wherever it was, it was something bad, for Ma begged and begged the men to leave them be, and it pained him inside to see her cling to their arms like she had no pride at all.

After dinner two rough constables came to take them out of there. They could bring nothing except what they wore, some tallow candles for light, and pots for cooking. "No bedding; 't'will be tainted,' no clothing; 't'will all be burnt,"–only a clean sack was given to them for provisions. They had little left in the larder, so the sack was half-empty.

The men tried to drag Da out by the feet, but Brendan put a fist into a man's jaw, so they shackled Brendan and dragged him outside. That made him lace up his mouth. Ma and Patrick followed, protesting and making a mighty fuss. In the fray, Da was forgotten.

They'd never been anywhere without him before. He'd brought them here to Scotland, right across the heaving Irish Sea. "A better life," he'd said.

Finn twitched back the curtain, hoping to see Da get up, and greet for his ale and bread as usual, but the bedchamber was fearful silent.

He whispered "Da?" But Da stared into the corner as if he wasn't there. It didn't look like Da anymore. Not like someone you could hug and jostle with; this stiff stranger. Finn's chest felt crushed, like a smashed bird's egg under a boot.

A shout of his name. "Finn!"

Ma. He hurried outside to the cart, scared he'd be left behind. It was already full. Women wailed and men dabbed at them to quieten them. They all had sacks like the one Ma'd been given, only theirs were bulging. Ma ignored the staring crowd on the street and grasped Finn's hand, walking through them, as they parted for her. They had never done that before, and it made her look like a queen. But a sad one.

The driver gave them papers; each a separate one, with a date stamp and a seal. Finn couldn't read what it said, but he was glad to have a grown man's quarantine paper just like the rest. He stared at it until Ma took it off him to keep it from getting sodden in the drizzle.

Two pikemen hauled the city gate open to let them pass, and then shouldered it shut as the cart rolled out, under the blackened heads on spikes, stark against the cloud.

The town faded to a distant grey blur, and on the cart folk fell silent, with every person trying to squeeze away from everyone else, not wanting to touch. A distant dog howled. They weren't all poor, Finn noticed. One old gent opposite him had silver buckles to his shoes and a silver mounted sporran. He caught Finn's eye and gave him a sympathetic smile.

Finn looked away, wishing Da was there.

After twenty minutes of bumping along the track, they came to marsh and moorland. By then, it was dusk and the city was a crouching hump in the distance.

"Yon's the place," the driver said through his thick muffler.

Animal pens, Finn thought. For pigs maybe, or hens. A long fence with huts behind. A gate with a bigger hut and two more constables stamping their feet and glowering at them.

"Another batch, Mr McPhail." The driver called.

"Aye. I can see that." The kilted constable raised his bushy brows at his friend. "More'n yester, too. Well, keep them away from us."

"Everyone out," shouted the driver. "Make sure ye have your papers. You're forbidden the city or to travel abroad without them, and they've been stamped. After a month ye can go home." He grinned, showing yellow stumps of teeth. "That's if you're still alive."

"Where are the houses?" an old woman asked.

"There. Yon huts will give ye shelter. There's a few unoccupied if ye be quick."

Finn looked to his Ma, but she was rooted to the ground.

"I'll get us one, Ma." Finn said. He set off down the dark track.

Most of the huts had a candle lantern outside, burning a smoky blue flame. From one of these came guttural groans, over and over. Finn skirted it and chose one that was in darkness.

The door gave under his push, but he couldn't see much. He felt a bench nailed to the wall, but no other furniture. A good den. Except that it seemed fearful small for the six of them. Five. He corrected himself. Da would've been too big for this place. He sniffed; the place smelt bad, like the slurrymen's cart.

He ran back and pulled on Ma's arm. "I've got one!"

Brendan was picking a fight as usual, with the driver. "We're not staying in this piss-hole. C'mon Ma, we're leaving."

"Then you'd be fools," the driver said. "Constables have orders to shoot or hang anyone who tries to leave. Yon's the gibbet, up the hill."

They all turned, unable to resist a look. The shape of it sobered them. There was already a man swinging there.

They huddled in the cramped space as rain trickled through the roof and down the walls, making a wet pool in the middle of the earth floor. Finn drew his feet under his backside. Now they were all here, Da's absence shouted to be heard.

"How will they bury him?" Ma said.

Brendan shook his head. He'd stopped his bluster. Patrick, never one to move quick, leapt up and ran outside. They heard him vomiting and a dark chill lodged in Finn's stomach. He crept close to Ma and tried to nestle in her skirts, but she showed no sign she knew he was there. She had turned dumb and her hands that were always busy with weaving and cooking were still.

The next day Patrick did not rise from the floor where he was sleeping. Ma turned frantic, running hither and thither for help, but none came. By evening Patrick was dead. The vice in Finn's chest tightened.

They took Patrick away that evening. The dead cart passed along the main track with a ringing of a bell. Ma and Brendan carried him out; Brendan hitched him under the arms, and Ma held his knees. Patrick's feet swayed stiffly. He had big feet for thirteen years old, and his soles were black and calloused with walking. A weight like a stone crushed the breath from Finn's chest so he could barely breathe.

Ma's nails dug into his hand as they followed the cart to the pit. The old gentleman with the buckled shoes was there too with a long sad face, staring down into the hole. The stink made Finn gag. They weren't going to put Patrick down there, were they? Finn wanted to have a deek, but the old man pulled him back.

"Don't look, lad. T'is not a sight for thee." He turned to the carter. "Can I say a few words?"

The carter said nothing but sucked more furiously on his pipe.

They tipped Patrick in, and Ma let out a long wavering wail that made Finn's insides turn to water and his eyes smart.

The old gent spoke some words from the Bible, but Finn barely heard them. A terrible thought had just struck him. Hadn't Reverend Fett told him thieving would bring plague and pestilence on their houses? A cold wash of guilt made him feel in his pocket. The locket was still there.

It was his fault. The realisation made his knees buckle. The fact that his Da and Patrick were gone was all his doing. Tears pricked at his eyes. He blinked, but they trickled down his cheek anyway. He dashed them away with his sleeve. He'd have to make it right and take the locket back. Soon as it was light, he'd go.

Finn stood out at the front of the hut and surveyed the camp. The gibbet, now empty, loomed on its slight rise in the distance. Finn took a deep breath and darted towards the fence that ran along the edge of the field, noting where it became bog and marsh. He'd left Brendan; big, loud-mouthed Brendan, curled like a babby on the floor, groaning in pain. He'd die, Finn knew, if he didn't do something. God took one of them every day.

The long fence was patrolled by two kilted constables armed with muskets. *I could climb that, easy,* Finn thought. As he watched, the plague cart returned, bringing another batch of people, who gazed in disbelief at the scatter of huts, and covered their noses at the stench from the pit.

One of the constables spotted him. "Awa' with you, little devil!"

Finn pretended to be deaf like he did with Ma, and walked towards the end of the fence. A deafening bang. Instinctively, Finn threw himself on the ground. Behind him cold earth splattered over his shoulders. He rolled over to see a cloud of smoke just behind him.

Jesus! They'd actually fired at him. The musket ball still smoked in the turf.

"Get away from that fence!" the constable shouted. "It'll be yer hide, next time!"

By now the noise of the shot had brought every fit person out into the open.

"Finn! What in the name of Jesus d'ye think y're doing? Get back inside this very minute." Ma powered towards him, her mouth in a small bunched O of anger. She grabbed him roughly by the shoulder and slapped him so hard across the back of the legs it made him yelp. "Haven't I enough grief to deal with, without you get yersel' shot?" She took hold of his wrist so tight he thought it might snap, and dragged him to the hut. There, she bade him strip off his shirt, and turn about, and drop his breeks to his knees. "You don't feel sick?" she asked.

"No, Ma."

"You're not to go near anyone else, hear me? No one." A whack across the ear. "And stay close, so I can see you, or I'll kill you, so I will." Then she seemed to think better of it, and held him so tight his ribs hurt. "Sorry lad, I'm so sorry."

"Is it Brendan?"

She didn't have to say anything, just looked down at him with eyes too swollen and red to cry.

First Da. Then Patrick. Now Brendan.

Finn saw the pain in the hunch of Ma's shoulders as she walked into the hut and guilt gnawed in his belly. He'd done that, with his sin. In darkness would be best. He would go tonight. God would probably make him die the last, just to punish him.

The night was starless, with a mizzle to freeze the bones. Finn crept past Ma, who was huddled with baby Ruari close to her chest. A lump rose in his throat. His family was so small now; the hut seemed a big empty space with no big brothers to fill it. He pulled on his muffler and his Ma's mittens that were worn to rags at the fingers and felt in his pocket again for the glass of the locket.

The surface was smooth as ice in his hand. He shoved it back with loathing, and latched open the door, hoping for a moon to light his way, but the sky was dense with cloud. He kept low to the ground in a half-crouch, and scuttled towards the boundary fence. There he paused, watching for the guards. He'd seen them earlier, as they strolled up and down and stopped for a pipe at the gate. Two pinpricks of red and two wisps of sideways-blowing smoke showed him their whereabouts.

I'm putting it back, d'ye hear? He cast his eyes up to the heavens and imagined a vengeful presence staring down. But he kept going, fear coiling up his spine, away from the gate along the fence, until his feet felt the squelch of marshier land, and his nostrils smelt the brackish bog beyond. Water pooled up to his ankles, and icy mud oozed between his toes. He turned, to glance back and to his horror, the guard was coming his way, steely helmet bowed against the rain.

Finn dropped lower into a crouch, hiding his face in his hands.

A few yards away came the splat of boots and the tang of pipe-smoke drifting through the drizzle. He heard the man stop at the point where the fence stopped to give way to the marsh, and willed him to walk back, but he didn't; just leant his back on the fence, his face turned out to Finn.

Finn dare not budge, though his feet were numb and his teeth chattered. He clamped them together and tightened the grip on his ribs. His fingers shook with cold.

"See anything, McPhail?" The other constable called.

"Nah. Was probably a stray dog that escaped the cull."

"If you see it again, yell, and we can both take a shot."

The guard laughed and walked back towards his friend. Finn unfurled himself to upright. He couldn't walk for he was stuck knee-deep in peaty water with legs that seemed to belong to a different boy. With an almighty effort, he dragged one foot free, but then toppled. The splash was too loud to be ignored.

148

A crack behind him. Frantic, he elbowed his way on his stomach. More cracks, explosions that sent showers of mud over his shoulders. Finn dived behind a patch of reeds and lay still, panting with effort. He felt in his pocket for the locket, and hung it on its chain around his neck. He feared to lose it under the seeping water. The firing had stopped. They'd need to reload, he realised.

Grabbing the window of time, he leapt to his feet and pelted as fast as he could, half-tripping, half-leaping over the marshy land until he could see the fence had run out, and he could run past it, through the marsh, towards where the lights of the castle in the distance flickered on the rock like tiny stars.

Over by the fence, the constables peered into the darkness. "Shall we go after him?" McPhail asked.

"Nah," Stirling said. "If we do, we'll be abandoning our posts."

"He'll not get far anyway. Someone else can—" He stopped mid-sentence. A woman was haring towards them, out of the dark, skirt flapping.

"Have you seen a boy?" she panted, barely able to catch breath. "About so high, hair like a fox?"

"Aye, too right we've seen him."

"Praise Jesus! Which way did he go?" Her glance raked beyond them up and down the fence.

"Nearly lost his head, the little scoundrel," McPhail said. "He's awa'. Couldn't stop him. He's out there, somewhere." He gestured over the fence to the no-man's land beyond.

"You let him go out there? All alone?"

"We fired on him, but he wouldn't stop." Stirling folded his arms, defensive.

"You fired on him? A small boy?"

"We had to," Stirling said. "It's orders. He could be carrying the disease."

"Let me past." She made as if to push by, but McPhail

swung up his musket. It stopped inches from her chest. "Keep back."

She baulked, but then stuck out her chin. "Let me by."

"Orders are to hang those that try to leave. An' if I remember right, you've a babby back there that needs you, so you'd best think twice on't."

She faltered, took a step back, her face crumpling. "What would you do?" she yelled. "What would you do if it was your son?"

"He'll come home, lass," Stirling said. "Boys are always running away."

"Call this home?" she gestured behind her at the ragged row of huts. "You don't understand," she said, her voice breaking. "He's seen his two brothers die here! He'll never want to come back."

Finn's breath rasped in his throat as he pushed onwards towards the hulk of the castle on its cliff. Beneath his feet the track grew stony, and glimmers of light illuminated the Flodden Wall, with the Nether Bow Gate yawning like a giant's mouth. A knot of armed men guarded the opening.

Finn stopped. There was no way to approach without being seen, but there was no way to go back either. He hadn't planned it properly, he realised. He'd only thought as far as returning the stolen locket and not how he'd get back to Ma once he'd done it.

What would Da do if he was here? Likely cuff him round the ear, and tell him he was an eejit. The thought of his Da made him brave. Behind him, a clack of hooves on stones and rattle of wheels grew louder. Immediately he dropped flat on his face in the shallow ditch beside the track.

The horse shied, sensing him there, but the driver applied the whip and the undercarriage rumbled past his vision. A miller's cart, he guessed, by the spray of dust dropping onto the track. Just ahead of him at the gate, the cart stopped and the driver dismounted to show his papers.

Now! Finn scooted up behind the cart to climb in, but the miller walked around the side to check the load, and Finn had to dive for cover. He winced as his knees scraped the dirt, but took firm hold of the long pole that joined the two axles and clung there, terrified someone would peer underneath and see him.

The cart shook and shivered, for the horse sensed him and was restless.

"Whoa, Captain," he heard the slap on the horse's neck, and the miller's floury boots appeared briefly beside him before they stepped onto the running step and the cart creaked away. A jolt and Finn held his breath, hands numb with clinging on. He clamped his feet tighter round the pole to retain his foothold as the cart jounced down the cobbled streets.

Just a bit further, he thought, *get out of sight of the gate.* He could see nothing but the underside of the cart, so he counted to a hundred; *one Hail Mary, two Hail Marys, three Hail Marys,* until he got to forty-nine and unable to hang on, dropped to the ground.

"Hey you!" The miller's sharp cry.

But Finn was already running, legs weak as feathers, bobbing and weaving down the wynds.

At the end of the street, he stopped and put his hands on his knees, to curb his shaking breath and the stitch in his side. This part of the town was brooding and full of dark shadows; lanterns were unlit on houses, and shutters closed as he hurried down the narrow passages towards the tenements of Burgh Street. As he spotted his own house, he could not resist taking a deek. To his surprise the door was open. Maybe Da wasn't dead after all, maybe...

A dark cross stained the door. Inside, the house was a skeleton, just bones, with all the flesh stripped from it. No curtain, no furniture. Even the loom had gone and the wooden shelves had been torn from their brackets. He didn't know absence had a smell until that moment, a sour scent of sadness that made his mouth quiver.

He turned and ran. At the end of the street his tenement

castle reached towards the sky and Finn hurtled inside, up the stairs, round and round the stairway. Somehow he'd imagined the door he wanted would be open like before, but of course it was shut and the corridor dark. Like his own house, the door had been daubed with a red cross. The paint glistened red in the meagre light, and pinned to it was a notice, but he couldn't read what it said, just saw that there was a signature and it had the stiff look of officialdom about it.

Voices and footsteps. Finn bolted past the door, leaping up the stairs two and a time. Below him, he heard the door open and close and men arguing. It seemed to go on, with voices protesting, before the scrape of a trunk on the stairs.

He waited until it was quiet before descending the two flights to the door. He knocked softly, in the gap between the paint, his ear close to the lock, listening. Nobody came, so he knocked louder. Was the lady at home? Still no answer.

He tried the handle, not expecting it to turn, but it twisted easily in his hand and the door creaked open. To his surprise, the sconces were lit, and a branched candlestick flickered on the mantel. The woman's portrait was gone, leaving a light patch on the wall and the same empty silence as in his cottage.

Hearing no sign of life, he went into a bedchamber, but it was empty, with a strong medicinal smell, though the sheets had been bundled in a heap in the corner, and the side table bristled with bottles and salves. A leather travelling bag lay on the mattress, gaping open. Finn stared at the collection of objects inside; a watch, some silver spoons, coins, a gold snuff box, a woman's jewellery.

He knew instinctively that this was loot. Someone was burgling these people. Momentarily he felt outrage fill his chest, until he realised he was a thief, too, and remembered why he'd come.

Disgusted with himself, he hurried back towards the parlour, took hold of the locket, and was about to unloop the chain from around his neck when two figures burst back in through the door, heaving a trunk between them.

"What the—?"

Finn stopped short in the doorway of the bedchamber.

"You little thief!" The biggest man's eyes fixed on the gold chain in Finn's hand and he crossed the room in three strides and made a grab for him, "Give me that!" Finn knew him straightaway, the constable with the bulbous nose, the one that had turfed them out of their cottage.

"No," Finn cried. "I've got to put it back."

"Give it over!"

"Wait a minute, Bill," the thin-featured man near the door said. "We've seen him before. He's one of those Irish we cleared out of the cottages. I remember his red hair. They got taken to Boroughmuir."

"You mean...?" The man called Bill nodded and the two men backed off.

"I only came to put this back, sir," Finn said. "Reverend Fett said God would send the plague to thieves and sinners. And now near everyone's dead."

The men looked uncomfortable. Bill seemed to come to a decision. "You were looting. Give me that."

"No!" Finn made to run past him, but the other man raised his gun and the next moment a blow hit him on the crown of the head. Finn fell, the floor rushed up to his nose, and stars exploded into sparks on his eyelids.

"You fool! You've killed him." The voice seemed to come from far away. "What the hell were ye thinking?"

"He was looting."

"And we weren't? Why'd you bludgeon a bitty bairn?"

"He'd tell on us."

A sigh. "Bloody fool. Quick, take this sheet. Wrap him up. The dead cart'll be along soon to carry him away. They'll just throw him on with the rest."

"What about the gold round his neck?"

"You can touch him there, if you want, I'm not. Not worth the risk."

When Finn woke, he fought for air. His feet dragged over cobbles, a cloth was swaddled around him. He struggled to free his arms. A cry of alarm, and then he was suddenly dropped. He battled his way out of the sheet to see two ragged men staring down at him.

"This one's alive!" one of them said, revealing stumps of teeth.

Coughing, Finn rolled over. He felt his head. Blood oozed from a flesh wound under his hair. He prodded it with his fingers. A proper wound. His brothers would be amazed. And then he remembered, with a spasm of pain, only Ruari was left.

"Don't touch his skin! He looks in a bad way. And live ones have to go to Boroughmuir," the man said.

Finn groaned. Boroughmuir. Where you went to die.

Rough hands bundled him up in the sheet again, and next thing he knew, he was on a cart again, jammed on the floor against the clogs and boots of the other passengers. His head ached and the passing landscape was hazy. A great wave of tiredness washed over him. He was still a thief and he could never put it right. The locket was still round his neck, like a noose.

Maveen Gallagher was waiting hollow-eyed by the gate. She'd watched every cart come in, gripping her rosary beads in her hand. As this one trundled up, she scoured the people, looking for a glint of red-hair.

No sign. Until a white shrouded figure rose up from the bottom of the cart. "Ma!"

She'd kill him. He was waving crazily, like it was all a big adventure, and not like he'd put her through hell at all. She charged towards the gate. "Finn!" she yelled, "get down off there. Wait until I get my hands on you, you little rat!"

His face broke into a tearful grin and he tumbled off as soon as the cart was through the gate, trailing a bedsheet, and dodging her slappings before she enveloped him in her arms.

He pushed her away, unsteadily, eyes full of worry. "Ma, where's Ruari?"

"A gent agreed to mind him whilst I met the carts. How could you? Where the hell have you been?"

"Ma, I went to find our house."

"Aw, Finn." She blinked back tears and squeezed him tight, ruffled his hair. A yell of pain.

"What is it?" she was suddenly afraid.

"My head. I hurt it. I fought off two robbers and one hit me with a gun."

"Don't tell lies." She slapped him across the backside. "And don't you ever do that to me again. What on earth will I do with you?"

When Finn arrived at the hut, it was to find the old gentleman with the silver-buckled shoes dandling baby Ruari on his knee.

"You remember Reverend Johnson," his Ma said.

Finn went and put his finger out and Ruari caught hold of it with a surprisingly tight grip.

"He's a fighter, your brother." Reverend Johnson said.

Finn just nodded. His head still hurt. Ruari started to grizzle and Ma took him outside. "He needs feeding," she said.

Reverend Johnson was grave. "Best stick together in times like this. Your mother needs you. What made you run away?"

Finn squirmed. "It's my fault. My fault my brothers died."

"No. How can it be your fault? They died of the plague. Like my housekeeper."

"Because the preacher said if I was wicked, God would bring a plague to my house."

"Did he indeed? So you were wicked, were you?" He

looked amused, though his eyes were still sad.

"Why are you laughing?" Finn was close to tears.

"Can I tell you something, Finn?" Reverend Johnson patted the space on the bench next to him, and Finn sat. "I'm a preacher, too, and I tell you preachers don't know everything. We're not God. But I know this: if you think your God to be vengeful, then that's what he is, but if you think him to be merciful, then so he is. The world has ever been a mixture of joy and sorrow."

"But I was a sinner. I stole something." He let the words gush out in a torrent. "And I wanted to stop the plague so I tried to take it back, but I couldn't, so God will always be angry, and folk will keep on dying, and I'm afeared that Ma ... that he'll take Ma next." He screwed up his face to stop the tears which poured hotly down his face.

"What did you steal?" he asked gently.

Finn yanked out the locket from beneath his shirt, and pulled it gingerly over his head. "This. It was from the big tenement house on Bankside." He stared down at it. "I don't even know why I took it."

Reverend Johnson turned it over in his hand. He seemed to think for a moment. Then he smiled at Finn. "It looks familiar," he said, tapping the back of the locket. "Why, this is exactly like one I gave my sister."

"Do you live in Bankside?" Finn asked. "The end tenement, on the fifth floor?"

Reverend Johnson nodded.

"Open it!" Finn jumped up in excitement.

"Oh, there she is," he said, pointing at the portrait as he turned it over. "Would you ever believe that!"

"Really? It's really her?" The gentleman was smiling at him in an indulgent way. "What's her name? Will you give it back to her?"

"When they let us go home, yes."

"But I went all the way to the city!" And the gentleman listened as Finn told him everything. "Tell your sister, I'm sad I couldn't put it back, and I'm sorry for taking it."

"Well, it's back where it belongs now." Reverend

Johnson slipped it over his head. "And you've had quite an adventure, haven't you? But you can rest easy. You've done everything you can to make things right. You're a brave lad. A good lad. And I'm sure if God's watching, he'll know what you did, and he'll keep you all safe."

"You're sure?"

"Aye."

"And you're a real minister?"

"Aye, for my sins, I am."

Finn felt his shoulders drop, and his head rise as if a great cloud had fallen away. At the same time, he felt wobbly as a new-born calf. He ran outside to find Ma. Maybe she could fix his broken head.

A month later Reverend Johnson stood at the gates of the city, his papers in his hand. He was thinner, and his hair greyer, and the buckles on his shoes had lost their shine. But those were small things compared to the fact he was alive, when half the city was dead.

The guard at the city gate examined his papers, and keeping a wary distance, waved him through. Reverend Johnson walked slowly up the hill, marvelling at the absence of horses and carriages, the lack of droppings in the gutter, and the echoing silent streets. At the top of the hill near the castle, he gazed down at the dark chequered pattern of houses below, and wondered where it was that the boy, Finn, and his mother and the baby had lived.

They were going back to Ireland, she'd said, where their memories were still shining ones. He was glad they had survived. Had he done the right thing? He felt for the locket around his neck before walking up to the house next to his kirk. He stood a moment, happy to see the familiar stone-built vicarage with its low roof.

He wished them well, wherever they went. A person had to have hope to survive, and, so help him, he had wanted to take some of the weight from that boy's shoulders. What a tale he'd told! Had it been true, or just fantasy? The lad must have a good imagination.

But then, he thought to himself, he'd told his own tale. He had never had a sister, and the people in the tenement–whoever they were–would never get their locket back. He would keep it, as a reminder to preach well. And his lies had served a bigger purpose, given hope to a boy who was trying to make sense of the fact he'd lost a father and two brothers, within the space of a few days, and who badly needed something to believe in. And in the end, he was sure, it was hope and kindness and stories that kept you alive.

Inspiration of Deborah Swift's The Repentant Thief

The Edinburgh plague of 1645 is the worst that the city ever experienced, with about half the population losing their lives, and three thousand dead in the port of Leith alone. Cramped living conditions (as seen on a 1647 map) led to a rapid spread of the disease. In a brutal measure to contain the contagion, sufferers were forced into primitive huts outside the city, where they could await their fate. Burgh Muir (modern spelling) was one of the places were huge burial pits were dug for the victims. Such was the fear of the disease that, according to Robert Louis Stevenson's *Edinburgh: Picturesque Notes*, those who concealed their plague symptoms were punished. Women were drowned in the quarry holes and men were hung and gibbeted in their own doorways. The cause for the disease was uncertain, so it was nearly always attributed to God's vengeance against a sinning people. See my article, "Health and Hellfire," in *Historia Magazine*. This was the idea I wanted to explore in my story, "The Repentant Thief."

Learn more about Deborah Swift at http://www.deborahswift.com

Arrows that Fly in the Dark

By Katherine Pym

London Estuary
7 March, 1665

Sixteen-year-old Gabriel Wicken-Smythe stood on the main deck of the *London* as it sliced through heavy swells in the Thames Estuary. Next to him, and garbed as a lad, Samantha Mercy-Simpson leaned over the rail, her brown, shoulder-length hair blowing in the wind.

She had appeared from the future in a maelstrom of colour to land on the planks crowded with goods, livestock, men, and women. Translucent when she plopped in a flurry of arms and legs, only Gabe could see her as his hand passed through shimmering flesh and bone.

Now, fully in this time, she pointed at the birds that swept about the masts and laughed. "We're up so high."

He smiled. Lovely to look at, he could not fathom why others did not recognize her for the lass she was. He extended his hand to the protective mist that shrouded them in a gauze of comfort. During his time travel, he'd always felt safe within its folds.

"Where did you say you are from?" he asked.

"From the twenty-first century in America." She looked at him. "And you are from where?"

He grinned. "I was born in 1935, Chester, England."

"I'm fourteen and will be able to do this until twenty-five."

"Same here," he said with a grin. It would be fun to travel with another.

She raised her head. "Let's go up top. We'll feel like soaring birds." She clambered to the poop deck.

He laughed and followed where the winds buffeted. Atop

the roundhouse, so high he could almost touch the low-lying clouds, he breathed in the magnificent beauty of the world.

"I've always hoped to ride the oceans in a ship of sail." He pointed to the masts where men scampered like ants along the yards.

"I'm very glad I had a chance to see this," Sam confessed.

They were on this ship's maiden jaunt after being retrofitted for war with the Dutch. Headed for the small town of Deal, Gabe expected to be put ashore with the rest of the guests.

"How did you come to be here?" Samantha demanded.

His mode of time travel hung from a leather cord around his neck, a dull, ugly thing and hardly worth a thief's sleight of hand. From what he could see, Sam wore a necklace of lacklustre design similar to his own.

He opened his shirt to show her his. She nodded, her eyes bright with acknowledgement.

The deck rocked beneath their feet. "What the devil?" Gabe exclaimed.

Sam twirled about.

A concussion rumbled deep within the ship, fought its way to the top and rippled the boards of the main deck. Fire burst from the prow. The hull ripped open and cannon crashed into the sea. Burning and broken bodies, arms and legs flew out then plunged into the estuary.

Another eruption cracked the bowels of the ship, broke her back, twisting the forward half to the left while the aft soared toward the sky. Sam cried out and flung her arms around Gabe as a firestorm blew from the hull.

As if waiting, the *London* faltered for a moment, then another blast reverberated through her. It hurtled through the hull, ripped open the decks.

Gabriel wrapped his arms around Samantha. Their pendants touched. Mist shrouded them as they flew into a vortex of safety.

160

Prismatic shards of light sucked them into a tunnel of energy. Vibrations throbbed until Sam's skin rippled, her eyelids fluttered. She tumbled through spirals of time.

With Gabe's arms around her, the flow seemed sluggish. Foreign scenes had not the clarity or colour as in her earlier travel. Voices still burrowed in her mind but of seventeenth-century England.

Suddenly, quiet heat engulfed her. Terror and woe filled her soul. With a sob, she fell onto a dirty lane, the shadows deep from cantilevered houses that swelled over the narrow road. Nearby, Gabe toppled to the ground in a gangly pile.

The world smelled of simmering rubbish. A woman sobbed. Someone groaned.

She stood and brushed off her breeches. Her coat that was far too hot in this summer's warmth. With a grunt, Gabe gained his feet.

"Where are we?" Sam asked when he drew near. She gasped at the rats that foraged in a pile of rotting food debris. "Are we in a ghost town?"

His gaze searched the area that seemed desolate. "`Tis London, methinks." He scratched his head. "Awfully quiet, though."

"There you go again, speaking funny."

"What do you mean?" he demanded. "You speak thusly. `Tis the way of the mist to protect us in all things, including speech."

"I speak as you do?" She hadn't listened to herself but now she would and was about to say this when several people rounded the corner. They strode with purpose toward them.

Sam stepped closer to Gabe. "Who are they?" she whispered.

"Not sure." He pushed her behind him, but the people did not bother them. They continued to a house down the lane. A wooden sign over the lintel swung in a puff of breeze. *Mister Hodges, London Physician.*

"Let us follow them," Gabe murmured. "See what's afoot."

Sam kept close to him when they walked through an open door into a large front room, where people sat on benches set against the walls. Many groaned or rubbed their heads in abject misery. One person vomited into a deep dish, his face full of agony.

A narrow man in a brown doublet and breeches entered the chamber. Clean shaven, his tawny hair was shorn above the shoulders. Spectacles sat on his nose, secured with ribbons about the ears.

He gazed at those in the chamber, his eyes settling on Sam and Gabe. "Where have you been? Most of the day is taken. Come, there is a patient I want you to see." He turned back whence he'd come as if expecting them to follow.

Gabe regarded Sam, his eyes filled with question.

"Don't know," she mouthed.

He shrugged and followed the man into a corridor where they hit a curtain of sharp odours: cloves, cinnamon and fennel. An open box sat in an alcove, its lid against the wall.

Gabe's feet stalled. Sam looked over his shoulder. A preserved corpse of a young boy rested in a coffin, the flesh shrunken and browned as if he'd been slowly baked in an oven.

Sam's throat closed. Tears welled. "I've never seen a dead person, before." *Why am I here? What does the mist want me to learn?*

"What date is this?" Gabe asked the retreating back of the physician.

"'Tis fifteenth of September 1665. Why do you waste me time with useless questions?" He wandered around a corner and they stepped quickly after him. "The weekly *Bills of Mortality* hath said more than eight thousand died of the plague last week. We must do something to restrain this woeful tide."

"Let us help him." Gabe nodded with enthusiasm.

"I'm not sure that would be a good idea. We could get sick, too."

"Not with the mist protecting us."

Samantha frowned. "I'm not so sure about that."

They entered a chamber permeated with the smells of pharmaceuticals. A large table filled the space. Black rats roamed the skirting boards and sniffed the pungent air.

"Have you had your daily antipestilential electuary?"

Eyes wide, they shook their heads. Sam did not know what an electuary was.

Hodges picked up a large bowl and stirred a thick paste with a wooden spoon.

Gabe looked doubtful. "What's in it?"

"What has happened since last eve?" Hodges looked hard at Gabe. "You act as if this is new to you." With a smaller spoon, he scraped a dollop of the paste and handed it to Gabe, then did the same for Sam. "Now, put this on your tongues. Let it soak into the mouth, slide down your gullet and lodge into your heart."

Gabe stared at the lump of red paste that began to ooze. He bent closer to Sam and whispered, "I've accepted worse from our chemist's in Chester. How bad could it be?" He slurped it onto his tongue. "Why is it red?"

Sam grimaced.

Hodges clicked his tongue. "Why do you not know this? You've made the medicine often enough. It comes from the fluid of crushed *kermes vermilio* scales, found in the land of our Lord."

Gabe gagged. "You mean the worms found on the Palestine oak?"

Sam's belly heaved. Ugh, bug juice. Gossamer tendrils of mist caressed her. She tentatively tasted the potion. "Hmm, nutmeg's one ingredient. Not too bad."

Hodges scowled. "You will swallow all of it, or not go on rounds today. 'Tis made of the green rind of walnut, figs and plums, a bit of vinegar, Virginia snakeroot, nothing that will harm you."

Sam grinned. "Virginia? As in the colony of Virginia?"

He glared at her. "Put the paste upon thy tongue, lad, or thou wilst be the sorrier for it."

How could she have forgotten she wore boy's garb? Her throat in a knot, she scraped the paste with the edge of her teeth and let it fall on her tongue. "Horrid."

"Now, come with me." He walked through an open doorway where a child of about ten lay on a narrow cot. His chest distended, he laboured to breathe.

Hodges took the youth's limp arm and pressed his fingers to the wrist. "The arteries hardly beat. I believe in a few short moments we shall lose him to the heavens." He tucked the child's arm under a sheet. "I prescribed scordium water three hours hence, and repeated it recently, but as you can see, he continues to struggle." He gazed at them, one of his eyebrows raised toward his hairline. "If'n you remember, scordium is a plant with healing properties."

His explanation helped somewhat, but Samantha did not know what he wanted. She bumped against Gabe, who shrugged.

Hodges huffed a breath. "I know not what happened to you in the night. `Tis as if you went to bed me `prentices and returned changelings. I'm quite minded to charge thee with witchcraft, but our health situation is too dire. I require thy assist."

Sam's heart beat erratically in her chest. She had read of the Salem witch trials where illogical beliefs had killed many, mostly women. Suddenly, wispy veils soothed her ruffled spirit. The mist would protect her from harm.

Gabe squeezed her hand. "It is hard to think with so many dying about us."

"You have seen worse in weeks' past and should be used to it by now. If you wish to apprentice with me, put iron in your backs." He stepped to a dresser with open shelves that held stoppered pots. "We shall apply a plaster. Come."

Samantha and Gabe stood around the cot. The lad's face was blue, his breathing erratic.

She touched his forehead. Very hot. Aspirin and

antibiotics would help enormously. Were there equivalents here, three hundred years in the past? She studied the chamber for a plate of mouldy bread.

Hodges chose a large pot and removed the stopper ringed with wax. He plunked it on the table next to a stack of small linen squares. "You will apply this onto a cloth. Be generous then press it to the youth's swellings." He pointed. "His neck, underarms, and groin."

Neither Sam nor Gabe moved.

"I shall strike thee with me willow-wand if you do not attend right this very minute."

He's vexed and Sam's eyes widened. Now, why had she thought that particular word when she never used it in the whole of her life?

Gabe took a cloth and scraped salve onto it while Sam gritted her teeth and removed the blanket. The boy's face and chest dirty, he could do with a good soak. It would, at the very least, keep down the infection. She wondered why their arrogant physician never thought of that. She glanced at the doctor's fingers, their tips covered in ink, the nails encrusted with dirt. What a terrible time this was.

Gabe applied salve to the lad's neck. Sam raised his arm and he applied the plaster to a swelling there. She slid the blanket down to expose the boy's nakedness. She closed her eyes whilst Gabe applied the chunky cream.

"Uhm, sir." His voice cracked. "We've something here."

Curious, Samantha opened her eyes.

Hodges sniffed. "The discolouration indicates a raised blister with a loss of sense very near to spacelation." He rubbed the bridge of his nose, the spectacles rising and falling. "Gangrene, young persons. Gangrene. Mister Gabriel, please apply the plaster to the infected part, whilst I fetch a pigeon."

"A pigeon?" Samantha cried. "Whatever for?"

He glowered, his hands clawed as if to choke her. "Do not vex me with thy questions. Once more and I shall throw thee on the street."

Afraid the physician would strike her, she stifled a cry.

Gabe pushed her behind him, his body stiff. "We are full of sorrow so many have died and cannot think of anything else," he said.

The physician's eyes brightened. "Ah, thou hast the strange vapours of the brains due to the great sadness in this world. Now, I understand and will give thee a moment to gather thy wits. But only a moment. We've too much to do for thee to be coddled."

Gabe gave Sam a squeeze of encouragement. Sparkling vapour burrowed about her neck, seemed to brush moist kisses on her cheeks. She stood taller, hoping to have enough strength to continue.

Hodges sat a dead bird on the table. "We shall apply this to the bottom of the youth's foot but not to draw away pestilence. Due to a profusion of pores, this pigeon will send warmth through the skin and keep the animal humours more flexible. It will stay the person's natural heat within the confines of the skin."

Sam's resolve to be strong crumbled. She could not imagine this would work and was about to say something when Gabe shook his head.

Hodges nodded at Gabe. "Tie the pigeon to the God-foot."

He hesitated.

"The right foot," Hodges derided. He crossed his arms over his chest and studied them with a gimlet eye. "The left hand and foot are the devil's talons and must not be used."

Gabe affixed the dead bird to the bottom of the lad's right foot while Hodges flicked the blanket over the youth's chest. "We shall repeat the application of plague water before going to infected houses. The spirit of the pestilence has a terrible, fiery nature that disperses through the body due to its great volatility. The healthful drink will correct the malignant quality of the pestilence within."

Sam turned to Gabe and mouthed, "What did he just say?"

He grinned.

"I must say you are treating this as a great lark." Hodges

plucked up the pot and stoppered it, then replaced it on the shelf. "People are dying and the Court of Aldermen has appointed four physicians to take care of the entire town." He shook his head and began to mumble. "We shall prepare to visit the sick. Get thy plague clothes." He wagged a finger. "But afore you do this, have Cook pour us each a cup of sack."

"I am thirsty," Samantha confessed. With all the windows closed, it was hot in the chamber. "Could we open a window?"

Hodges yanked the spectacles to his forehead. The ribbons tightened, bringing his ears forward. "And allow in the poisonous miasmata to taint our spiritual humours? Nay, I say! All who enter this chamber would die."

"But—"

Gabe knocked into her. "I shall go to Cook whilst you fetch the plague cloaks." He motioned toward a wall with clothing hung on pegs. A narrow bench nearby held hooded masks formed like birds' heads, narrow brimmed hats attached. Rounds of glass protruded from the eye holes.

"Don't forget the boots," Hodges said. "Remember, Mister Gabriel, you untied yours from the long breeches which must be reattached."

"Aye." Gabe paused, his hand on the door. "Where is the kitchen, again?"

Hodges scowled.

"I shall find it." He hurriedly left the chamber.

Not sure this garb would save them from bouncing fleas, Sam wondered which was hers. With one arm, she swept the bundle from the pegs, some waxed leather, others stiffened canvas. With the other hand, she piled the bird hoods on top of each other, noting gloves in their hollows and carefully lugged everything to the table. "What sort of leather is this?"

"'Tis Moroccan." Hodges selected tinctures, bottles and pots then set them in an open box.

"You mean from Morocco? 'Tis a long ways away,

methinks." Her skin prickled as she listened to her words, their inflection. But for the timbre, she did not recognize her voice.

"Nay, you silly person," Hodges cried. "Goat leather is called Moroccan."

She mentally shrugged and dumped the pile on an empty portion of the table. *I'll be miserably hot in this.*

She ran back for Gabe's boots. One moved. Gingerly, she picked it up, a toe wiggling. She dropped the boot and squealed when a rat scampered out.

Gabe returned with a tray of horn cups. "Cook says this is made of the best ingredients."

Hodges continued to pile medical supplies onto the table then line them carefully in the open-lidded box. "I shall use myrrh today, a very proper thing. Where are my lozenges of treacle and sour grapes? I cannot lose those, for they are most dear and hard to come by now most shops are shut up." He took a horn cup from the tray and sipped. "Ah, this will warm the belly very well." He regarded them. "Well, go to, go to."

Sam recoiled, for the taste of the electuary still lingered on her tongue. She had learned in science the combination of drugs could cause a negative interaction, resulting in harm or death. She guessed the man did not tell them all the ingredients and she did not want to take the risk. "Are you sure these medicines won't cause mischief within, sir?"

The physician did not heed her but drank deeply from his cup. He swallowed and sighed. "I am a follower of Anthanasius Kircher, who wrote of tiny worms, the propagator of the pestilence that kills so thick around us. Our cloudy country will not allow me to see them, even under the best of glasses, but I believe, as does he, these little worms enter through the pores and invade the blood to cause sickness. These medicines we take will keep the worms from entering our pores." He finished his drink and foraged through the plague robes, separating each.

She grabbed a waxed leather gown and breeches with boots attached. They both watched Hodges strip off his doublet then step into the boots, raise the leather to his waist and snugly tie the cord. He swept the gown over his head, the long skirts flowing to his boots.

Gabe shook out the waxed canvas. He secured his boots to the bottom of the breeches with leather string, then followed Hodges' way of doing it.

Sam regarded her long breeches that rumpled at her ankles, the boots huge. *I've enough room for another set of feet.*

"Have you shrunk overnight?" Hodges smiled as he slung a pungent sack onto the table. He plunged his hand into it and brought out a fistful of spices, dried flowers and leaves, then dumped it into the beak of the bird mask.

Gabe and Sam did the same.

Hodges removed his spectacles, pinched the beak, and slipped the hood over his head, rounded glass protruding through the holes where his eyes should be. The little hat wobbled on his head. He straightened the cowl that draped over his shoulders and onto his chest.

He released the beak and took a deep breath. "Now, we are ready to visit the sick." His voice was muffled as he waved his thickly garbed arm. "We haven't all day."

Sam struggled into the plague gown. She pinched the beak to keep spices from rolling out and slid the hood over her head. Her eyes did not meet the mask's glass.

The combined odours, with camphor and myrrh amongst the most pungent, seared her brain. Eyes watering and the hood black as pitch, she wheezed and felt jittery as if she would soon faint.

She pulled off the hooded mask, spices tumbling out, and threw it on the table. "I cannot do this." She leaned over the table and gagged.

"You will not soil me wares. Go outside if you must spew."

Gabe picked up her mask and stuck his finger in the holes of the beak. "These were stopped up, not allowing you to breathe. It should be better now." His smile did not hold humour.

She shook her head.

"I shall be right alongside you." He pinched the beak and settled the hood over her head.

Holding her breath, Sam stared out the wavy, glass eyes that showed a distorted chamber. *I'll die in this.* She breathed in spices but they weren't as strong as the last time.

"Come along, young 'uns." Hodges grabbed hold of a long wooden stick adorned with a metal beak, barbed strings attached. "Mister Gabriel, do take the carrying case." He rounded on Sam, his mask's beak brushing her head. "What shall I do with you, Mister Samuel? You seem too frail, today, for proper business."

"I shall be fine, sir," she begged, not wanting to remain behind. "I'll take notes."

He waved a gloved hand. "Ah then, very well said. Grab those loose leaves and inkpot. Off we go. The afternoon flies, and I shall have me supper."

Gabriel kept an eye on Samantha buried in the strange plague garb, but like a warrior, she shuffled along, holding the skirts of her gown above the dirt. He caught her when she stumbled over a broken paving stone, or wandered too close to a mouldering cesspit.

"Thanks," she said. "I can't see a thing in these slops."

Gabe laughed. "Slops, like used clothing?"

"These are definitely used. Horrid. I can't breathe, either."

He pulled her to a stop and rearranged the hood. "Can you see and breathe, now?"

Her shoulders slumped. "Yes, although I'm not happy about it."

The lanes were empty of folk. Rats scurried under piles of dried muck. Pigs with their ribs showing rooted in shrivelled rubbish.

"This public pestilence came to us from Holland." Hodges waved his staff as if striking the distempered air. "Before that, it came in bales of cotton from Turkey, which is a strange preserver of the pestilential streams."

Samantha cocked her head. "What did he say?"

"I know not. Most of his speech is gibberish. I'm glad he doesn't speak to us in Latin."

Hodges pointed his stick at a house. "We shall stop here." The front door bore a red cross with words roughly scrawled beneath it: *Lord have mercy on us.*

"What does it say?" Samantha leaned forward as if trying to decipher them through the hood's rippled eyeglasses. "Oh dear." Her voluminous pile of clothing shuddered.

Nearby, a guard sat on a joint stool, two of the legs up as he leaned against the wall. The stench of death drifted from the windows and half-oak timbered walls.

The stool legs landed with a thump when the guard stood. "All gone here. The dead-cart is on its way." In the distance a small bell rang as wheels trundled over cobblestones.

Hodges adjusted his plague mask. "We shall move on then. Good day to thee."

The guard nodded and returned to his stool.

"I thought the carts came in the night," Gabe remarked.

"Too many dying, sirrah. They come all hours, now." He shook his hooded head. "What did the devil's imps do to me apprentices? I heard nothing in the night whilst you slept." He waved his gloved hand. "Come along, then, come along. There's a house down here where the family took extraordinary precautions and voluntarily shut themselves in. We shall see if they have need."

They came to a large house, its frontage made of stone with a wide porch, a makeshift closet at one end to protect the watchman in all weathers. A tin duct rose from the little shelter, up the outside wall of the house to a shuttered first-storey window.

Gabe pointed. "What's that tube thing?"

The physician scowled. "If you waste my time asking foolish questions, I shall strike thee. `Tis for the rope and pulley, to safely bring food and whatnots up and down." He stepped to the porch where the closet door stood ajar. The leather hinges squeaked in the hot air. "Oiy there, Mister Milton, art thou well on this bright day?"

The shutter cracked open, a flash of gunpowder exploded, its smoke billowing down the tube. A little scream emitted from Samantha's plague garb. "What was that?"

The physician tsked. "`Tis to fumigate and purify the air."

"Is that you, Mister Hodges?" A man's voice rolled down the tube. "We are well but wonder at our porter gone missing these past days. Have you seen him?"

"He is not at his station, Mister Milton."

"I am most discouraged, Mister Hodges." The man's voice echoed. "We constructed this contrivance to keep the illness away. Nothing should cling to the tin walls but apparently it does. We've lost the person who runs errands for us, fetches letters from the posthouse." He paused a moment then cried, "We are alone without any news of the outside world."

A woman staggered up the lane, her arms crossed tightly about her belly as if in great pain. A thin man trailed behind her. "I have come to tell you that your porter is dead."

"Who are you?" Milton shouted down.

"I am his melancholy widow."

"Nay." Milton's voice cracked as if greatly affected.

"You are ill, Mistress," Hodges stated.

Gabe's heart sank, for he had never been so close to death. He remembered World War Two with clarity, the rationing, the wireless that reported countless bombings in London and Liverpool. On clear nights, he and his mum stood outside and watched the skies flash over Liverpool, felt the ground rock under their feet with the bombs' concussions.

"Mister Gabriel, the medical box if you please."

Gabe started, then he remembered where he was, in London during the height of a pestilence. Sam's plague mask faced him. He envisioned her frown under the stiffened leather.

"Here, sir."

Hodges took the case. He placed it on the porch and opened the lid.

"What may I do for thee, good lady?" Milton's voice blared down the conduit.

"Dear sir, I am well taken care of by our Lord. He has touched me with the distemper and I shall soon follow me husband."

Hodges took her arm and pulled her to the porch.

"I have sinned, sir. Please whip me with thy staff and banish me sins."

"I cannot, Mistress. If you were at the start of this disease, I would, but now you are too weak. To strike thee would be to murder thee. This I cannot do."

"Why did you come if you are ill unto death?" Milton implored, the fear in his voice blaring from the chute.

"I have brought a good man to take my husband's place, sir," she replied. "He will serve thee as my husband had."

"He could carry the pestilence, Goodwife. I shall not endure it."

She shivered and coughed. "But he is safe, sir." She succumbed with a sigh to Hodges' ministrations.

He motioned for Gabe. "'Tis a terrible slaughter we are seeing. Remove the blue pot from the medical box."

"Corpses are everywhere," the lady muttered. "Tonight, I shall be one of them."

"Nonsense," Hodges cried.

"How is this new man safe, Mistress?" Milton demanded.

"I have lost strength," she whimpered. "Please tell the master this man has had the pestilence and is recovered a fortnight. He will not get it again."

Hodges stood. "I have seen this phenomenon." He

penetrated the man with a studying gaze. "I've also seen where they fall ill again," he quietly said so that only Gabe and Sam heard him.

"But he comes with you, who are infected." Milton's stubborn tone flared. "I shall not touch anything he handles. He must be approved by the parish constable with another to vouch for him afore I shall allow him near me door, or in me closet."

The good lady whispered, "He will be honest."

Gabe closed his eyes, for the woman wilted like a flower under the heat of a flame.

"Fetch the pesthouse cart, sirrah," Hodges instructed the new fellow. "What is your name?"

"Harold, sir."

"Harold, then, run afore she dies before our very eyes."

The man took to his heels whilst Milton slammed shut the window. A puff of gunpowder smoke drifted down the pipe but overwhelmed by the spices in his mask, Gabe could not smell it. The dark cloud drifted away in the soft breezes.

Hodges stood with resignation. "We can do no more."

Sam and Gabe followed the physician, who headed for another lane. After they rounded a corner, they came upon an empty street. Deadly quiet, the sun beat down on them. Grass grew between the cobblestones and birds trilled from the porch roofs.

Suddenly, screams pierced the air. A guard shouted at a barricaded door. "Oiy then, Emmett, what goes on in there?"

From the inside of the house someone pounded on the door.

Hodges ran up the porch steps. "Let us in."

The guardsman shook his head. "Too dangerous."

"Aren't you here to attend these people, run errands and

the like?"

"Mayhap, earlier, but now everyone dies. I don't want to be next."

"Give me the key, then." Hodges menaced the man with his staff, the barbs swinging near his face.

The guard threw the key on the ground and ran away.

Samantha retrieved it from the porch stones made smooth by the scrape of feet over the years. "Here, sir."

"Many thanks to thee." Hodges inserted the key into a padlock and wrestled with it.

Shouts and screams pummelled their beings. Someone fell hard against the wall.

Hodges barged into the house, Sam on his heels, Gabe behind her. A man and old crone grappled on the floor. The woman's cap fell off, her white hair flowing about like attacking spectres.

"Stop this very minute," the physician cried. "You'll murder the old woman."

Emmett wobbled to his feet. Drenched in sweat, his odour was pungent. He groaned and staggered backward. Holding his head, he landed hard on a stool. "Me head hurts terrible and me heart thunders in me chest but I do not have the plague."

"How dost thou know this?" Hodges derided.

"A-cause I've the clap. `Tis well known plague will not attack a poxed person. Went out special to a filthy slut after the first *Bills of Mortality*."

"Why would you do that?" Gabe asked, his tone astonished.

Samantha could not fathom the stupidity of such an act.

Hodges staggered to a stop. "You have mouldy brains to think such. Venereal buboes transition easily to pestilential carbuncles, sirrah."

The sweating man moaned. He started to remove his dressing gown. "Come see the carbuncles. They are of the clap, not the plague."

Mister Hodges turned to the old woman as she gained her feet. "Art thou a filthy nurse trying to steal from this good man?"

"She tried to strangle me whilst I slept," Emmett cried. "Me treasures are at the bottom of the stairs."

"Indeed." Hodges menaced the nurse with his staff, the sharp barbs banging on the stick. "I've seen work from your kind. You strangle patients or lay distemper upon them. You plunder the dead." He jabbed her with the staff's point. "May divine vengeance strike terrible retribution upon thee."

She backed away, shaking her head.

The sickly fellow groaned. "Mayhap, I should have awaited the plague. This clap sickness is horrid." Emmett began to slip off the stool.

The man's heat permeated Sam's plague suit that she knew would not protect her.

Emmett scraped his teeth over his black tongue.

Sam gagged.

"I'm very dry and need a drink but everything comes back up." The poor wretch slumped to the floor in stupefaction.

"Misters Gabriel and Samuel, make the poor wretch comfortable. He is too far gone to climb the stairs to his bed. Cover him with a counterpane." He turned to the nurse. "Have you tainted this poor devil with your evil?"

Frail and thin, she shook her head; her hair flailed about. "I have not."

"I loathe your type." Hodges pointed to the open door. "Get out!"

She limped away, her bony fingers curled. Cackling, she staggered down the lane.

Emmett sat up, his eyes glazed, his cheeks flushed with heat. "I am well again. Fine as fettle." He blinked. "Look at the flies in the lane, buzzing about in the kennel. They are big as rats. The rats are big as bears."

"'Tis the atmosphere filled with pestilential poisons that make these things large." Hodges struck a pose. "Although I must admit sometimes a very subtle aura is mixed amongst the poisons, loaded with gross and sulphurous

176

particles and perceptible to the senses." He stared out the door. "But today I see none of this."

Sam sniffed at the physician in his Moroccan plague suit, his little hat wobbling atop his head. She did not understand a word he said as he enlarged upon his theories, but it did seem he enjoyed the sound of his voice as he rambled on.

Emmett tried to tear off his dressing gown. "I'm so hot, I cannot breathe." He gasped. "I'm going to be sick." Vomit spewed across the chamber.

Samantha stumbled over the long plague gown and yanked it to her knees. She dashed outside to the porch.

"Turn him to his side," Hodges ordered as he snapped open his case and rummaged for a medicine. "His lungs are distempered. I expect him to go into hot sweats. If they have a cadaverous smell, we shall know if he will soon climb the holy stairs to heaven."

"He smells of death, sir," Gabe said.

Sam tried to breathe. More than anything, she wanted to remove the suffocating hood with its obnoxious smells. She'd never be able to abide the scent of camphor or myrrh again.

"Mister Samuel," Hodges called to her. "I shall have thee assist. We will evacuate pus from the buboes."

Gabe lay on top of Emmett, who writhed beneath him.

"I cannot hear you, nor see you," Emmett cried. "I am now deaf and blind." Tears ran unchecked into his hair.

The physician uncorked a bottle. "Prayer and fast will help thee, sirrah."

A cart trundled by. "Bring out your dead. Bring out your dead."

Everyone gazed at Emmett who seemed very alive at the moment.

"Raise his dressing gown," Hodges ordered.

When Gabe slipped off the poor fellow, stark hopelessness gripped Sam's soul. Horror filled her gut. Plague would find her; kill her before she reached adulthood.

Wisps of the gossamer veil wound about her, soothed her and spread peace. Her vision cleared and she sighed.

The man's upper thighs had large inflammations that looked very painful. The skin tented with mounds of puss, the flesh around it red as if burned. Some were black and gangrenous.

"Is it scurvy?" Emmett breathed, his face twisted in agony.

Hodges knelt beside him. "Hast thou been to Holland? Scurvy coalesced with the plague in Holland last year."

Emmett gasped and lay his head upon the floor.

Hodges poured fluid from the bottle onto a rag. "We do not want scurvy to join the plague which is called *outlandish scurvy*."

Emmett panted. Stinking perspiration drenched his person.

Hodges tsked. "Have you applied a cooling cataplasm?"

Emmett's eyes opened but Sam saw he was blind to all but the pain that consumed him.

"Mountebanks sell cataplasms but do not direct one how to use them," Hodges continued as if in a lecture theatre. "This carbuncle must be scarified. We shall hope to alleviate the pain and death of the flesh about it." He set the bottle and rag aside and wagged his hand. "Bring me the medical box."

As Hodges held a knife to the sunlight filtering through the shutters, the blade flashed. Emmett started to scream.

Two days later, Gabe staggered down the stairs, his face flushed, his eyes glassy. "I could not sleep last night. Too many dead-carts, their bellmen calling to bring out the dead."

Sam sucked in her breath, fearful he had the onset of the plague. "Do you have carbuncles in the folds of your legs and arms?"

He collapsed onto a stool. "Aye, the start of them."

Urgency filled her, stripped her soul of peace. "We must get you to a doctor."

He chortled, his laughter more like gasps. "We reside with one."

"I mean a real doctor, one with antibiotics or whatever they do to make the plague go away."

Her limbs shook and her lips quivered. "We must get you home, right now."

He put his head in his hands. "When is home?"

"2020."

"I cannot go forward, only to my time of 1951 or backward."

Samantha felt dizzy. "Did you have antibiotics then?"

"Yes, we do." Gabe rocked and moaned. "But I don't know if they work against the plague."

She stood. "Then I shall go to my time and bring back the proper medicine." She motioned to the chamber. "Not any of this quackery."

"Quackery?" Hodges voice filtered to them from his laboratory. "Who blasphemes?"

Sam hugged Gabe. "I shall be right back. Please don't go anywhere. I must be able to find you upon my return."

Gabe sighed. "I'm too ill to move."

Sam would have privacy and ran up the stairs to the garret, their sleeping place the last couple of days. She grasped the pendent and thought of her mother, her dear Gran. "Return me to Mom and Gran. To Mom and Gran."

The chamber dimmed. Prismatic shards of light sucked her into a tunnel of energy. Vibrations throbbed until her skin rippled.

She tumbled through spirals of time. Foreign scenes flashed across her vision. Voices from other cultures burrowed into her mind. Winds shrieked and a tree fell somewhere in the woods.

Sam flew through the wall into her grandmother's attic to find Mom and Gran. A storm raged outside.

"Oh my goodness, you've returned to us. Thank the

Lord." Mom visibly calmed, her eyes pricked with tears. "Where did you go?"

"No time. I found a friend and he has the bubonic plague. He couldn't come with me. I must find a medicine that will cure him." She started to weep. "I can't let him die."

Gran hugged her. "Don't fret, sweet girl. We have what you need."

Mom searched through a box filled with bottles and vials. "Here it is, doxycycline, first manufactured in the 1940's. It could upset his stomach and you may think he's worse." She handed Sam the capped bottle. "You will not be immediately encouraged. Patience is important."

Sam took the bottle. She quickly kissed Gran and Mom, then imagined Gabe in the physician's house, ill and in great need of help.

Colours circled her as a vortex of time and noise from the centuries swept her off her feet. She landed with a whoosh onto the wooden plank floor, Gabe on a truckle bed.

Patience, she repeated in a mantra as her body and the bottle slowly materialized. The moment the meds were hard and real, she unscrewed the top and dug into it with her fingers. "You need something to drink with this."

"There's a half-cup of sack over there." He tried to raise his hand, but it flopped back onto the bed.

Sam studied the room, turning around and finally saw it, a small horn cup next to rags and tincture bottles. She grabbed it and handed Gabe a pill. "Down with it."

He swallowed it then heaved a breath. "There, I feel better already." He lay back on the bed, panting.

She did not like this. *We must leave this plague time.* She knelt next to the bed, tucked the bottle in Gabe's doublet then pulled him into her arms. Their pendants touched. Winds blew against them and they were whisked away into the mist.

Inspiration of Katherine Pym's
Arrows that Fly in the Dark

Nathaniel Hodges, M.D., and fellow of the College of Physicians, was indeed a real person who remained in London during the 1665 plague and lived to tell of it. He was born (14 September 1629) into a large-ish family and attended Westminster School. He won a scholarship to Trinity College in Cambridge, then transferred to Oxford, where he finished his schooling as a physician in 1659. He died in debtor's prison, January 1688.

Medicine as seen in this piece is correct. Science was burgeoning, but their tools were still too primitive for total understanding. The magistrates of London forced all dogs and cats killed as they may have carried the contagion. Considering the fleas that lodged in the fur of these animals, this shows how close to the truth they had come.

Even as Hodges followed Anthanasius Kircher, who wrote of tiny worms, the propagator of the pestilence that entered through the pores to invade the blood, current scientists wonder how he came to this conclusion when the actual particles are too small to have been seen by the microscopes or magnifying glasses of the era. Geronimo Fracastorius, a Veronese physician in the fifteenth century, is considered the first documented person to discuss germ theory.

Someone who came down with the plague could die in a matter of hours, or days.

The ship of sail *London* exploded on 7 March 1665 in the Thames Estuary. Only recently have experts come to the conclusion this explosion was caused by guncotton. Gunners reused old artillery cartridges, which were made of canvas and gunpowder. Over time, canvas cartridges deteriorated to a fine dust and when combined with sulphuric and nitric acids found in gunpowder, friction occurred. They became volatile. Spontaneous explosions of wooden sailing ships were reported throughout the seventeenth century.

Learn more about Katherine Pym at
https://novelsbykatherinepym.blogspot.com

778

By Melodie Winawer

Venetian-Occupied Greece
17th Century

The deck of a Venetian galley provides no shelter. Gripping our oars, sitting on rows of hard, backless benches, we are packed so tightly there is no room to stand. Sun beats down on our skin until we burn, then blister, then burn again. In the winter the rain soaks through our clothes. Sometimes the snow is so thick on my eyelashes I can barely see, but I cannot lift a hand from my oar to wipe it away.

Snow is rare off the Morean coast, in this land that belonged to Greece before our Sultan won it two centuries ago, making the Peloponnesus a jewel in the crown of the great Ottoman Empire. Now, the Peloponnesus belongs to Venice, as do I. Even without snow, the wind at sea lashes like a slave master's whip, and the cold numbs our limbs— though never numb enough to provide relief.

"What does it matter whether we can see; we might as well all be blind," the slave to my right said to me the day the snow came. He was Turkish, like me, and he whispered in our shared language, so the master would not hear or understand. *"What is there to see if our only purpose is to row until the flesh comes off our bones? We see only the world we cannot live in, the land whose shores we cannot walk upon, the liberty we have lost."*

I know the answer to that question now, but it took me years to find it.

A messenger knocked at the door of our house before dawn one spring morning in the year 1687. I was twenty-five then, a new husband and even newer father. I woke to see our tiny Behlil curled against Malike's side, as it seemed he always had been; the birth of a child changes not only the future, but the past. My son and wife breathed together as if they were still one being, one inside the other, and I inhaled the sweet air around them. Nightingales sang in the dark outside. That day, I believed they sang for pure joy, celebrating the new life that graced our home. Since then, I have learned that the nightingale sings all night to keep itself awake, for if it sleeps, it will be killed and devoured.

Our Greek servant, Makarios, answered the messenger's knock. From my bed I heard his shuffle, then the creak of hinges, murmured words. I met him in the hall, softly closing the door to the chamber where my family slept in their milky haze. In the kitchen, Makarios lit a candle from the night's banked hearth. I read the message, standing.

Makarios had been with me since my childhood and served in place of a father after my parents' early death. He welcomed Behlil like a grandson, and cared for Malike tenderly in the first hours after our son's birth. But something had changed in Makarios after his son Nikos was chosen for the Janissaries, the Sultan's select troops. He asked me at the time to intervene, to have his son released from military duty. I was a rising officer in the governor's retinue, following in the footsteps of my late father, and might have had influence to carry out his request. Instead, I counseled him not only to accept his son's fate but to welcome it, for being chosen as a Janissary was a great honor. It seemed clear to me then that Greeks, given the opportunity to serve the Sultan, should rejoice in their good fortune, as should their parents.

Makarios's face grew dark when I refused to use my

influence to keep Nikos at home, but it was not his place to argue. Though I did not feel I could speak of it, I mourned Nikos's departure. He smiled easily and laughed often, and even as a young child, he had offered help with every household task no matter how onerous or unpleasant. The house felt darker in his absence.

After Nikos left, I also no longer felt the warmth from Makarios that I'd once basked in. At the time, I thought he might simply fear, as all parents do, for his son's safety. But I was wrong.

In the candlelit kitchen, I read the messenger's letter. Makarios knew me well enough to read its essence reflected in my face.

"Bad news?"

"The Venetians have surrounded Mystras. We are under siege." Our walled city, the last of the Turkish possessions in the Peloponnesus to withstand the Venetian onslaught, perched high on the steep hill at the foot of the Taygetos mountain range. Having taken Mystras from the Greeks more than two hundred years before, we knew it was nearly unassailable. But a long siege could bring us to our knees.

I did not tell Makarios that the troops aiding the Venetian commander were Greek—six thousand Maniates hungry to take back their land from the Turks. I knew, even then, that there was a reason I should not tell my servant that Greek armies were allied with the Venetians in this battle. But Makarios did not need to be told.

"*We* are under siege..." he replied, slowly, dwelling on the first word. Almost a question.

Nikos was chosen to fight with a battalion of seventy elite soldiers against the massed troops that surrounded Mystras. He came home crowing victory, but with a festering wound in his side. A week later, he took his last breath. After that, Makarios hardly spoke to me at all.

Late at night, I confessed to Malike how much I missed Makarios, how I felt that now I'd lost my father a second time. Malike, with her usual wisdom, answered: "You are not alone in your suffering, Kadri. Makarios has lost two sons." I knew she meant that I was the second; she softened her barbed words with a gentle hand on my cheek.

As thousands of enemy troops spread outside Mystras's high walls, our crops died, the cisterns ran dry, and hunger was our daily companion. One day I saw Malike, her own ration forgotten, looking down at Behlil, who had fallen asleep at her breast.

Malike, who had not grown up with the plenty I was accustomed to, caught my eye and smiled, despite the gravity of our situation. "Ah, Kadri, now you see how the heart satisfies when the body cannot. Though the future may seem dark, the world still shines with light."

I embraced her, burying my face in her soft neck. The smell of her skin—musky and sweet—and the beating of her heart against my own, filled me as no meal ever could.

August baked the hills brown, and soon the entire Peloponnesus had been abandoned by the Sultan's commander of war. Surrender to the Venetians and their Greek allies was our only course of survival. On the day of the council of war at Corinth that would decide our fate, I saw a rat in the storeroom, twitching nose buried in our last sack of barley, his paws ruffling through the grain.

"Makarios, we have vermin in the stores," I told him.

Once he would have bent his head to the task without question, but that day he answered: "What would you have me do?" He added a mumbled epithet, under his breath, in Greek. It was the first time I'd heard him speak his native language in my house. I did not understand the words.

I told him to kill the animal. He did as I asked while I watched, first with a trap and then a hard blow to the head. He used a hammer meant for carpentry, shattering the creature's skull with deliberate savagery.

"It is done, as you asked, master Kadri bin Ahmed,"

Makarios said coolly.

I stared at the carcass of the rat, left to rot on the trash heap. I felt a hollow in my chest where Makarios's love for me used to reside.

The council at Corinth fared worse than I could have imagined. Makarios and I stood outside the governor's palace to hear the herald read the words of the treaty aloud.

"The Turks have held out to the last gaspings of the whole Kingdom and have therefore forfeited compassion." Makarios, at my side, repeated the words of the council like a dire echoing poem. The intensity in his voice chilled me, transforming the man who had once sung me lullabies and who had crooned my infant son to sleep into a stranger. I remembered him wielding a hammer, shattering the rat's head.

The next clause of the council was worse: *"From the Turks of Mystras, all men aged seventeen to fifty shall be sent to the galleys."*

I felt faint, standing in the baking heat in the treeless plaza, and in the reflex of my boyhood, I turned to Makarios for comfort, but he shifted away. I stared up at the high walls of the palace that housed our Turkish governor. The palace had once been Frankish, then Greek, and until this moment, ours. I had once looked upon it as a symbol of the Ottoman Empire's dominance, but now it seemed to mock our transience. For the siege had eaten away our strong foundation like termites chewing timber, invisible until a house rots and collapses, teeming with insects at its hidden core.

As the herald's last words rang out, I saw a hope, but so slim as to be laughable, if laughter is possible in the face of such despair. The terms dictated that we could buy back our freedom at the price of 200,000 reals: more than could possibly be amassed even if we all gave everything we had and then gave it all again. When I turned to Makarios, he was gone.

The governor's second in command had fallen ill with

flux from contaminated grain, and I was selected to join the delegation negotiating surrender to the Venetians. It was a chance to prove myself, to command as my father had. But more than my own future was at stake; if we failed in our mission, we'd row the rest of our lives as slaves, chained to oars for hours, weeks, days, months, and years, until we forgot our families' faces as the leagues of water stretched around us. If we succeeded, we might walk again in the company of those we loved, on blessed solid ground, *Insh'allah.*

The next day I set out with a group of Turkish emissaries to meet with General Francesco Morosini, the Venetian fleet's commander. That morning, Malike embraced me fiercely, so hard I could not breathe.

"I had a dream," she said, her fingers digging into my back. Malike did not often speak of her dreams—she was relentlessly practical and unlikely to indulge any musings, especially her own. "I know," she said, acknowledging my unspoken surprise. "But listen. I saw a man all in red: robes, hat, cape, boots—but the redness bled from his clothes to color first his hair, then beard, then face. And then it pooled below him like a lake of blood." My solid Malike was trembling so hard it made her teeth chatter. "I am afraid."

"Malike, if I had a terrible dream you would tell me that dreams have no place in the world of the living. And this morning, I am a man setting out on an important errand, and you are a woman who has given birth to the greatest gift of our lives." I kissed her soft cheek. Malike tried to shake off her fear, but the tension in her shoulders and set of her jaw belied her efforts. I, more susceptible to the dark miasma of sleep and the premonitions of evil it can bring, took care to hide my uneasiness. Malike let go of me and picked up Behlil from his cradle; he was just awake and crowing to be held. As I left, I caught sight of them together, framed in the doorway. Behlil smiled for the first time, dispelling my fear. I travelled with that smile in my heart.

Morosini's galley was anchored, along with the rest of his fleet, off the Maniate coast. The banks of oars seemed to beckon, the narrow wooden benches lined up in ominous rows. Deprived of our weapons by armed guards, we were taken to the captain's private cabin.

Morosini wore all red: the soft peaked cap set atop his long curling hair, his broad collar, and the heavy cape that he wore draped over his shoulders despite the heat. Even his boots were red. Beside him curled a cat, white below and black above, and he stroked her fur continuously while she purred and pushed her head against him. I could barely breathe in the close quarters; the airless heat was stifling.

A translator was present to ensure that we understood one another, for we had no common language.

"I am proud to speak on behalf of the Turkish residents of Mystras, grateful to have been given the opportunity to plead our cause."

Morosini's attention seemed directed more at his cat than at me, but I continued, trying to keep my gaze steady upon him, though mostly I saw the top of his head with its red cap.

"Two hundred thousand reals per person being an impossible sum, we propose..." Here, as the translator pronounced the Venetian words, Morosini looked up from the cat, his hand lifting, almost in threat.

He said a single word I did not understand, but I could tell he was angry. I hastened to finish, guessing he'd stopped on the word "impossible" and might be about to run us through with the sword whose decorated pommel glinted at his waist.

"We propose an alternative we hope you will find acceptable, and in the end, of greater value to your excellency." Morosini's shoulders relaxed as the translator continued, and his hand returned to the cat's caress. I returned to our appeal with relief. "We, the Turkish residents of Mystras, formally surrender to Venetian rule. And we will, upon your agreement and issuance of the

189

order, depart from our homes, leaving behind all our possessions and not only the town of Mystras to your governance, but the whole of the Peloponnesus. It shall all be yours, if we are allowed to go free."

Morosini made a noise, somewhere between a grunt and a cough, but did not speak. I continued to read, keeping my voice as steady as I could. "All this we shall leave behind: shops filled with goods from many lands, bolts of silk, the palaces and mansions of the wealthiest men, churches decorated with fresco and mosaic, jewels passed from one generation to the next, the icons of our faith in graven silver, groves of olive and lemon, and, the houses in which we live. If we are allowed to walk through the Monemvasia and Napflion gates carrying only our children in our arms, then all that remains within the walls of Mystras and throughout the countryside shall be yours."

Morosini picked up the cat and cradled it. His cabin barely held our group of five men, and only the commander had space to sit. The galley rocked on waves we could not see. *Insh'allah: let us all leave the water, and with our freedom return to the land.* I repeated my silent prayer as we waited, interminably. Finally, Morosini cleared his throat.

"This is a reasonable offer which I favor. Return tomorrow just after dawn when my scribe shall provide you with my signed acceptance of your treaty. Now go, all of you, before I change my mind." We fled, stumbling on the rocking deck, to rooms in a squalid harbor inn. It stank of rotting fish and the wine was thin and sour, but in our relief and joy we did not care.

Before I slept I penned a note to Malike and found a Venetian boy who, for my last gold coin, would take it back to her. As I wrote I could see Malike's thoughtful face, the curtain of her dark hair, her strong, competent hands.

My Dearest:
Morosini has accepted our plan for peace. Leaving our home and all our possessions behind is a frightening

prospect, but it is the price we must pay for liberty. We shall walk free with the hungry, desperate days of the siege behind us, and the fear of a life on the galleys will melt away as we head to our new life. You have helped me understand that the heart provides sustenance when there is none to be found elsewhere. Let the Venetians have the city. You are my home, more so than the walls and streets and buildings of Mystras, as beautiful as they are.

Your devoted Kadri

At dawn we returned to Morosini's galley. This time a brace of guards, faces covered with wet cloth that smelled sharply of vinegar and rue, herded us at sword point down to a bare cell in the hold.

"Your commander was in our favor yesterday," I began, "I am sure there has been some error..."

"No error," one of the guards said, in Turkish, though by his garments I could tell that he was a Maniate soldier. "The plan has changed. Pestilence has struck Mystras, and no one will take your dirty possessions or tainted homes. You are the Doge's prisoners of war, and Mystras is under quarantine." With that, he slammed and bolted the door of our cell, leaving us in the despairing dark.

Now, I had more to fear than stepping into the unknown with my wife and child. The Greeks call the pestilence *Panouklà*, the Latins named it *Mortalità*. But for me, *Veba,* the name for the scourge in my own people's tongue, carries the greatest horror with it. All men fear the pestilence. But today, as the door of the hold's cell slammed shut behind me, I knew the *Veba* would take more than its due. It doomed many residents of Mystras to death by contagion, but beyond that, it had destroyed our plan for peace. Any Turks who survived the *Veba's* direct wrath could look forward only to a life of slavery. At that moment I could not tell which was worse.

Days passed. In the dark we lost track of time, marked only by the arrival of buckets of water from which we drank desperately, and into which we emptied ourselves afterwards. I prayed for the lives of my wife and son, begging God to spare them, and to deliver us all to freedom.

Four buckets had come and gone when a guard dragged me by one manacled arm up a narrow stair to the foredeck of Morosini's galley. The light burned my eyes, and my legs were so stiff that I stumbled and almost fell. Makarios waited near the foremast, which rose tall behind him, its sail furled. His familiar face made me weep with relief. I could not raise my shackled hands to embrace my old friend, and the guard kept me from approaching closer with a cautionary wave of his sword.

"Makarios, you're a welcome sight. Please tell me news of Malike and Behlil. If the *Veba* is rampant, I fear for their safety."

"I left the city before the pestilence arrived, but your wife and child were not so fortunate." He paused and my heart felt as if it had stopped in my chest.

"Have you heard word?"

Makarios's mouth tightened in a grim line. "Both gone."

My limbs gave way until my hands, then forehead pressed into the oak boards of the deck. I wished I could stay there forever, inhaling the sun-warmed wood rather than hearing Makarios's deadly news. But the guard prodded me with his boot until I rose again.

"I shall pray for their blameless souls," Makarios said. in his face, I saw a new edge, like a recently-sharpened knife. "I heard they died quickly; at least God granted them that mercy."

"Have you come to bring me home to bury them?" I would risk death myself for a chance to see and hold their bodies again.

"I am not at liberty to do so."

"They have taken you as a slave?"

"I am, for the first time, truly a free man. But the Doge has claimed you as his hostage, Kadri bin Ahmed. And all the Turks of Mystras have been confined within the town, or quarantined on ships off shore. No one will be free until the contagion has passed."

"Why have you come?"

"I work for General Morosini now. Venice welcomes the allegiance of the Greeks of Mystras against our shared enemy. The generals have entrusted us with arms, and the task of keeping the Turks under watch. *"Turks"*—he'd said, like "livestock." And I was one of those *Turks.* Makarios had been almost a father; now he was my master, and a harsher master than I had ever been to him.

Why had I not seen the truth before? He had been a Greek servant in a Turkish home. Welcomed into our family and treated with generosity, he had never defied me to my face, but in this moment I saw his fervently held belief: Mystras was by rights his, not mine. And he would fight beside the Venetians to reclaim it.

"Now that you stand where I once stood, I will say what I never told you: Having my only child taken by force to join your Sultan's armies was theft, and murder. Nikos died in the service you called an honor, the service you would not spare him from. He died for your people, not his own."

I had no words to answer.

"Take him to the quarantined ships along with his compatriots," Makarios said, pointing at me and nodding to the guard who'd brought me on deck. "As the general has ordered."

I wished, then, to be home and dead beside my wife and child, but instead, I was a hostage in this floating prison, with nothing to do but recall what I had lost. The *Veba* took more than my wife and son. I believed it had killed my soul.

I stayed for six months on Morosini's ship. With the quarantine nearly at an end, my faint remaining hope for release died. From my guards I learned that Turkish resistance had arisen again in Mystras, and a stockpile of forbidden weapons found in the fortress on Mystras' hilltop, in defiance of the treaty we had signed.

Venice's revenge was savage and swift. Within days, I

and two thousand other Turks sailed on the ships that had been our prisons to a rocky island east of Napflion, where we were marched to a frost-bitten field. A Latin priest baptized us as Christians in defiance of our true faith, before 312 Turkish girls and boys were distributed as slaves to the allied officers. Makarios might have been among them, taking one of the weeping children to serve him as he had served my father, and then me.

We were next: 778 able-bodied men chosen for the galleys. That awful day I learned my first numbers in the Venetian tongue as we were counted aloud, one by one, and led to the ships.

The slave benches awaited us, the oars that would be our constant companions for the rest of our lives. The dark waters of the Bay of Tolos slapped angrily against the hull as we took our places, I and the 777 other Turks of Mystras who had lost all hope on this frigid January day. We were free of the *Veba's* contagion, but not its consequences. Suddenly a fellow Turk, Hamid, who had watched as his two children and wife were sold into slavery, walked to the ship's rail.

"Why live?" he cried into the wind, and, his tears mixing with the sea spray on his cheeks, he threw himself into the dark water. The other men echoed his refrain, and before guards could stop them, hundreds leapt over the ships' rails, vanishing under the waves. I was carried in the press of men, until I, too, stood over the water that would be my escape from a future in chains.

I watched as my countrymen jumped to their deaths. Before I could join them, the slave master's hand closed hard around my arm and pulled me to my bench, to the years of rowing that would mark the rest of my days.

I have revisited that moment again and again. Why did I hesitate when others leapt? Why could I not cross the line between life and death as my fellow Turks did? Was it cowardice? Weakness? Fear of God's wrath? I have had years to wonder, and now I believe I know. Malike once tried to teach me, when I thought hunger was the greatest lack I had ever known.

Someday soon my aging body will fail, for no man can row forever. Then, when I leave this life and its toils, I shall at last see my Malike and Behlil again, feel the warmth of her embrace and return his sweet smile. Until then, when I look upon the water that surrounds me, the water I should despise as the unbreachable wall of my prison, somehow I still see the beauty of the sun glinting along the crests of each wave. The deep is like the heart of a sapphire, turning turquoise near the shore. Dolphins surface, grey-white and smiling as they play alongside our galley's hull, acrobatic in their joy. The sky is a bowl of blue with seabirds arcing overhead and I live beneath its startling vastness. How can it be that in the midst of such profound despair I can still find beauty in the world, and live on, when everyone I love is gone?

This mystery could not be taken from me—not by siege, not by slavery, and not by the *Veba* itself. It took me many years to learn what Malike knew, but, *Insh'Allah*, I learned in time.

Inspiration of Melodie Winawer's 778

My first novel, *The Scribe of Siena*, delves into the mystery of Siena's particularly severe devastation by the Plague of 1348. That was one reason I was asked to join a group of talented historical fiction writers and contribute to this anthology about the Black Death. I had no plans to write about the plague again, and I was particularly nervous about taking on any new projects because I was in the middle of writing my second novel, which is about Mystras, the now-ruined city in Greece that was once the capital of the late Byzantine empire. I'd sold the unfinished manuscript and had a looming deadline from my publisher. But I really wanted to say yes to the anthology, and I'd never written a short story... I couldn't let go of the idea. So I decided that if I could learn something that would help me with my novel-in-progress, I'd do it.

In my research, I discovered that an outbreak of plague had occurred in Mystras during a particularly tumultuous period when the Ottoman Turkish domination of the city was threatened by a Venetian takeover. At first, the plague anthology project was just a convenient way of learning more about the history I was already studying. But like all stories, it quickly took on a life of its own.

Greece's last eight hundred years, and Mystras's history in particular, are a story of recurrent occupation: first by the French (Franks), then the Ottoman Turks, then the Venetians, then the Turks again, until finally Greece won back its independence in the 1820s—only to be occupied for a final time by the Nazis in World War II. This short story, "778," like the novel about Mystras, arose out of my desire to portray the experience of occupation firsthand, from a personal perspective. What does it feel like to be governed, ruled, or enslaved by people who take not only your land but your way of life, your children, and your freedom? The way the plague changed the course of Mystras's history in the seventeenth century gave rise to a particular story of occupation, in which the conqueror—the Turks—become the conquered.

In the process of writing, I also delved into something deeper and more personal, an experience I had twenty years ago that changed my life. At the time, my mother had been diagnosed with what should have been a fatal illness. In fact, she survived it, but at that moment I could not imagine she would. I was walking home from the hospital in despair when I looked up at the sky to see sun glinting through the trees. And the sight was beautiful. I could not imagine how it was possible see beauty in the middle of such misery. That experience, the impossible coexistence of my own despair and my joy in the beauty of the world, lies at the heart of "778." It is a story not just about one man's terrible tragedy, but about the resilience of the human spirit that allows us to transcend and survive grief and loss.

Learn more about Melodie Winawer at http://melodiewinawer.com

For Book Clubs

1)   What are your thoughts about this anthology?

2)   Did you have favorite stories within the anthology?

3)   What was your favorite quote or passage?

4)   Did you pick out any themes in the anthology?

5)   How much did you know about the Black Death in Europe before reading this anthology?

6)   Did this anthology alter your knowledge or thoughts about the Black Death in Europe?

7)   Did you have a favorite character?

8)   If you had a favorite character, what made you relate to them the most?

Thank you for reading.

CPSIA information can be obtained
at www.ICGtesting.com
Printed in the USA
LVHW050407030520
654900LV00008B/2009

9 781939 138217